Found, Lost, Found

Some Other Novels by
J. B. PRIESTLEY

J. B. PRIESTLEY

Found, Lost, Found

OR

The English Way of Life

HEINEMANN : LONDON

William Heinemann Ltd
15 Queen Street, Mayfair, London W1X 8BE
LONDON   MELBOURNE   TORONTO
JOHANNESBURG   AUCKLAND

First published 1976
© J. B. Priestley 1976

SBN 434 60365 1

Printed in Great Britain
by W & J Mackay Limited, Chatham

FOR

Susan Cooper,

with great affection

One

THIS SUMMER MORNING, Ivybridge was sitting behind
his desk and smoking a pipe, which he kept taking out
to give it a disgusted look. He was Chief Establishment
Officer of the Ministry of Export Development and
Promotion. He had thick eyebrows and a big nose and
looked vaguely like an admiral of about 1910. He was
beginning to search for a pipe cleaner when his secretary
arrived, carrying a file. She was a brisk but pleasant girl
called Madge Leeds.

'Mr Dekker is here, Mr Ivybridge,' she said. 'Do you
want the basic details?'

'What I really want is a pipe cleaner.'

'There are some in the lowest lefthand drawer—'

'Of course there are. Thank you, Miss Leeds. While
I deal with this pipe, you must sit down and read the
Dekker details in a low and agreeable tone.'

'Thomas Edward Dekker,' she began. 'Born Highgate
1937, father a doctor. Educated Westminster and Jesus
College, Cambridge—Economics and Modern History.

Board of Trade 1962. Home Office 1968. Transferred, 1971, to present post, Ministry of Export Development and Promotion. Commended earlier by Priorities Division, but since then some adverse reports. A personal note to you from the Permanent Secretary himself, saying, "This chap is either drinking too much or going quietly off his head—or both. Meadows is thirsting for his blood. See what you can make of him." That's all, Mr Ivybridge.'

'And enough. What do they think I am? A psychiatrist. Incidentally, some of you girls know about people, so what do *you* make of him?'

'Well, he does drink too much,' Madge admitted, 'but he's very clever and helpful—and a sweetie.'

Ivybridge relit his pipe, didn't like the taste of it, pulled a face at it and put it down on his desk. 'Well, send him in.'

Dekker was tallish, thinnish, carelessly dressed for a principal in the civil service, untidy without being at all scruffy. He had a long face, cleanly shaved, and unusual because it was rather lopsided.

'Morning, Dekker. Do sit down. How are you these days?'

Dekker gave this question careful consideration. 'I'm all right these days so long as I've a fair amount of booze.'

Ivybridge was expecting anything but this. 'Well— that's candid—'

Dekker smiled, a lopsided smile not without charm. 'I'm a candid type, Ivybridge. Let me explain. Do you remember those old stories about men—usually doctors —on the Gold Coast or somewhere like that, who had to

[2]

keep going on booze. Well, I seem to be one of those men.'

'Except of course you're not on the Gold Coast—'

'But somehow London now seems some God-forsaken place like that. Don't understand it, but that's how it is. I go between here and my flat, with a few double-gins inside me, as if they were a pair of bamboo huts. There isn't another steamer for a couple of months, and I'm waiting for news from home.' He pointed a long forefinger. 'It's a terrible thing, Ivybridge, to know you're at home and yet to feel you're waiting for news from home.'

'No doubt,' said Ivybridge, doing his best with this fantasy. 'You're not married?'

'I was. Divorce.'

'I see. Pity! So, in short, you're drinking rather hard these days.'

'Possibly. But I don't get stoned, you know. I do my work. I take just enough to keep me floating through the day.'

Ivybridge lowered his 1910-admiral's-eyebrows. 'But sometimes floating into trouble. There's a rumour that you told the Minister not to be *bloody stupid*.'

'Just a mutter. He didn't hear me. He only listens to the Permanent Secretary, who *did* hear me. This Minister, my worst ever, represents the new democracy. He's really a stupid shopsteward on stilts.'

Ivybridge pretended not to have heard this, though something flickered across his rugged face. 'Now look, Dekker, we're trying to be fair. You've done good work for the department in the past. We don't want to lose you, and you in your turn don't want to become an alcoholic. Why not see a good psychiatrist, get a note from him and ask for some leave? I'd back that.'

'Decent of you. But what do I do when I've got the leave?'

'Oh—come—come! Haven't you some interest—some hobby—um?'

'I had. Watercolours. That noble old English art,' he added warmly. 'But I decided I was no good and never would be. Any fool can do a *bad* watercolour, but a good watercolour is something else. Even when I look at mine—half-pissed—they still seem terrible.'

'You could travel,' Ivybridge suggested.

'Can't afford it. I'd probably be spending the equivalent of two pounds on a dubious dry martini. No, that's out.'

'But the drinking you do here must be costing you a pretty penny, Dekker—'

'Certainly. But I don't spend much on food, clothing, and rent, none of which help me to float along—'

However, Ivybridge was now scribbling on a pad. 'I suggest you consult this man, Dr Belham. We'd accept a note from him. A month's leave. Perhaps two, if necessary. I'll ring him to make an appointment for you. Got to take yourself in hand, you know, Dekker.'

'But which hand?' he asked, smiling. 'The one that's beckoning to the barman or the one holding the glass? Yes—yes—Ivybridge—not a good way of life—'

'Of course it isn't. Quite unreasonable.'

'Certainly. But then—how's yours?'

'You've made a point, Dekker. I've about nine more appointments, mostly unpleasant, before I see the Minister and the Permanent Secretary. I'll be lucky if

I get back home by eight, probably to find my wife has asked in some neighbours. And they'll all wonder why I'm so irritable when I'm paid so much to do so little—just drinking tea and yawning over red tape—Oh pop off, Dekker—and don't forget about Dr Belham—'

Dismissed, Dekker lingered in the little outer office occupied by Madge Leeds. They were friends and he had visited her there before. She was a girl, rare in the department, who could be friendly and helpful without expecting any sex in the relationship.

'How about this psychiatrist, Dr Belham?' he asked her.

'We've used him before. In fact once I had to call on him—for a report he promised. He's large, fat and irritable.'

'Not looking forward to him, Madge. Besides, it's a lot of nonsense. I'm a hardish drinker, no doubt, but a long way from being an alcoholic. They start at breakfast time while I never look at a drink before noon.'

'No, you don't need a psychiatrist, Tom Dekker. What you really need is a wife. No—no—not me. But I know just the girl, and she's already interested in you.'

'Then tell her to stop. I had a wife—and once is enough. 'Bye, Madge—and let me know when Dr Thing will be expecting me.'

Two

IT WAS TOWARDS the end of a warm day when Dekker found Dr Belham in the rather depressing Upper-Wimpole-Harley Street region. He was ushered into a room full of furniture too big for it. But then Dr Belham was almost too big for it: he suggested a giant spectacled roly-poly pud. He also looked tired and already out of temper. He put Dekker in one chair and himself into a larger chair, facing him and much too close—an idiotic arrangement, it seemed to Dekker.

'So,' said Dr Belham after consulting a note, 'here we are then. *You* have a drinking problem and *I* am at the end of a long hard day.'

'Too bad, Dr Belham. But we'll have to make the best of it.'

'I'm supposed to say that kind of thing—not you,' said Dr Belham irritably. 'Now then—a drinking problem.'

'May I make a point here, doctor. You call it *a drinking problem*. Probably Ivybridge did in his note to you. But

I don't see any problem. I've never suggested to anybody that I had a problem. I enjoy a fair supply of alcoholic beverages—gin, chiefly—that's all.'

'No doubt. But that can amount to a serious problem. Tell me, Mr Dekker—' as if he were about to play an ace of trumps— 'have you ever thought of yourself as a weak man?'

'Certainly. Almost all the time. How do *you* find yourself, Dr Belham?'

This was not well received. 'Mr Dekker, you're here to talk about yourself, not about me.' He was almost shouting but calmed down to ask, 'Now—what about your childhood?'

Dekker gave him a smile. 'Don't worry about my childhood. It was fine. I didn't hate either of my parents. By the way, my father was a doctor. Nobody was cruel to me. I'd all the affection a child needs.'

'Possibly. Possibly not. What's certain is your feeling of insecurity—'

'I'm not wearing that, doctor. I don't feel any more insecure than most people do. Less I'd say. What with everything costing too much—'

'Don't start that—' glaring at him. 'I'm well acquainted with all the problems of contemporary living—'

'You must be. Makes me wonder how our politicians have the brazen impudence to show their faces in public, after the screaming mess they've made of things. However, if I have a few gins, I'm all right. It's the difference between trudging across a heavy ploughed field and floating across it—'

'It's the difference between facing reality and trying to escape from it,' Dr Belham declared heavily.

'Can't agree with you there, doctor,' said Dekker cheerfully. 'I find it easier to cope with people and things, that's all. I'm not always losing my temper. Too many people are losing their temper. Some of the articles you write, Dr Belham, are far too bad-tempered.'

'Nonsense, man!' he shouted. 'I may take a sharp tone now and then, just because there's so much prejudice and stupidity about. Look at you—supposed to be coming here to consult me—'

'Doctor, we're neither of us at our best. You've had a long hard day. I don't like this room—and I need a drink. Look at the time!'

But then the telephone rang, and while the doctor waddled across to answer it, Dekker got up and made a few vague movements, wondering if there might be a drop of something in the place. Dr Belham was even angrier on the telephone than he had been with Dekker.

'Yes, yes, yes, yes,' he was bellowing. 'But don't make ridiculous excuses—you know very well I can't accept them . . . Come on Friday then, at the same time . . . Nonsense! This is your last chance as far as I am concerned. . . . No, no, no, no!' And he banged down the receiver, wiped his face, and looked at Dekker in despair. 'What were we saying?'

'We were saying,' said Dekker hopefully, 'that you'd had a long hard day and I needed a drink.'

'You shall have a drink. I too. Pink gin?' He gave a pull at what appeared to be two shelves of eighteenth-century masterpieces, revealing a small lighted bar, out of which he concocted two enormous pink gins.

They were now back in the same two chairs but in a different atmosphere, its shadows lightened, a pinkish world. 'Ever collected stamps, Dekker?'

'No, never collected anything.'

'Nothing like stamps. Very soothing.'

'Used to mess about with watercolours,' said Dekker, 'but I've given them up because I'm so dam' bad. But I must say you've a noble idea of a pink gin, doctor. *Salut*!'

After acknowledging this compliment, Dr Belham said, 'Not having a love affair, are you?'

'No. But when everything's nicely afloat, I sometimes imagine one.'

This restored the doctor to his professional status and immediately he became irritable again. 'Not good. Worse thing you could do. Either find a real woman or try to forget 'em. Not easy of course in a society that's over-stimulated sexually—'

'But is it, these days? What about unisex and all that sort of thing?'

Dr Belham made some impatient gobbling noises and then drank a lot of his monster pink gin.

For no particular reason that occurred to him, Dekker nodded several times, swallowed more gin, then said, 'By the way, have you always been short-tempered?'

'Always. After I took my medical degree. I thought a long course of psychiatry might calm me down and give me patience. Now I'm worse than ever,' he continued angrily. 'God in Heaven!—I feel like a man with a small shovel confronted by a dung heap five hundred feet high. Misfits inside this room, millions outside it—'

'We are living,' said Dekker, the gin smiling for him, 'in a garden of neuroses—'

'And we don't have to be facetious about it. What's

[9]

to be done with 'em? For that matter, what the devil am I going to do with you, Dekker?' the doctor roared. 'You don't want treatment, do you? Of course you don't. And I don't want you as a patient.'

'Quite right. You'd hate me as a patient—'

Dr Belham went to his desk and began scribbling away. 'I'm suggesting a few weeks leave, preferably spent away from your usual surroundings. What are they —where do you live?'

'I've two rooms on a second floor in West Kensington,' Dekker replied cheerfully. He finished his drink before going on. 'Moved into them as soon as I was divorced. One advantage of not being married, you can live in a dilapidated street in West Kensington, save money on rent, and meet a richer variety of people. I share a bathroom with two ballet girls and the gloomiest Italian headwaiter in London. Upstairs, there's a doctor who's been struck off the register and an old woman from Vienna, quite dotty. Below there's a drunken Irish journalist and—'

But Dr Belham had had enough. 'I don't want the whole menagerie, Dekker. You'll get your leave.' He began shouting. 'Try a few weeks in the country instead of brooding in pubs—damned idiotic places. Just sit quietly at night with a few stamp albums in front of you. A quiet life for a change,' he bellowed. 'Relax. Take it easy. Quiet—quiet—quiet—quiet!'

Dekker was not without a sense of the dramatic. He couldn't possibly make more noise so he answered in a whisper. 'You're absolutely right, doctor. I'll keep quiet. I'll go where it's quiet. I'll stay where it's quiet. In a few days you'd think I was a mouse.'

Three

THERE WAS A hell of a din. The room, fairly long but narrow and jam-packed with guests, was also hellishly hot. So Dekker after shaking hands with O'Morra, giving this birthday party, forced his way back to the open doorway, where he remained, not wanting to be seen leaving at once. Everybody was talking except three O'Morra chums, truly stoned, who were trying to sing 'Happy Birthday' without keeping to the tune and time of that detestable composition. Dekker had a large warm gin, the best he could manage, and though motionless in the doorway was now amiably afloat, gazing amiably at most of his neighbours, jabbering and sweating in there. But then somebody new arrived.

She was rather tall for a girl and very good-looking. She was wearing a flowered pink shirt and dark blue pants but had brought with her a brisk businesslike air and was even carrying a notebook. Behaving as if he were in charge of the party, Dekker gave her a fairly stern 'Yes?'

'I'm Kate Rapley,' said the girl. 'Working for the Community Research Social Science Council—'

'Why?'

'To earn my living—'

'The only possible answer. Thank you.'

She ignored this, and went on, 'We're doing a survey of community life in West Kensington—'

'Well, here's a hot little parcel of it. But I don't think I'd try to force my way in, if I were you—'

The girl took a look, pulled a face, and nodded her agreement.

'However, I'll do what I can to help, Miss Tapley—'

'Rapley,' she corrected him sharply.

'Rapley. Allow me to introduce myself,' said Dekker, floating away. 'I'm J. Carlton Mistletoe—the inventor. Perhaps you'd like to make a note of it—um?'

'NO, I wouldn't.' Not an encouraging reply, but he went on, vaguely indicating some of the people packed into the room. 'That fellow there is a millionaire property developer—he has two highrise office blocks without a soul in them—but he likes to come here pretending to be a drunken Irish journalist. Now those two, who look like ballet girls, are really the novelist, Antoinette Pewter, who writes all those very sad sexy stories, full of unmade beds. You know her work?'

'No,' said Miss Rapley. 'And I don't believe you do.'

'Quite right, I don't. Now over there is Madame Bovary—'

'*Madame Bovary*?'

'No, I'm sorry. Madame Ba-vo-ry. Ancient Viennese. She's a patient of Freud's who told him he was talking a load of rubbish—'

[12]

'And so are you,' said the girl sharply. 'Where's your room?'

'Floor above. Why?'

'That's where we're going.' She made for the stairs and he had to follow her.

As they climbed the stairs, dim and smelly, he said 'I don't know what you have in mind, Miss Rapley, but I wouldn't say I'm really in the mood—'

'Shut up and don't be silly.' She was sharper than ever. How could the Community Research Social Science Council ever survive her? But then why should it?

Arriving at his sitting room, cluttered with books, records, half-finished watercolours, she gave it one searching female glance. 'Squalid—even for these parts,' she announced.

'Miss Rapley, even now, I suggest, we must try to use words properly.'

'Don't be pompous.'

'This room is *not squalid*. It's damnably untidy, I'll admit, but that's quite different. I don't get much service. Remember, we're in the twilight of the English middle-classes—'

'Never mind about that.' She faced him. 'You listen to me. I'm trying to earn a living, not playing games.'

'But is there anything up here to suggest I can provide you with a living?'

She cut him short fiercely. 'Shut up! What d'you mean by offering me all that garbage downstairs? Do you think I'm an idiot? Because I'm not. And you're not J. Carlton Mistletoe—nobody ever could be—you're Tom Dekker at the Ministry of Export Development—'

He stared at her and couldn't escape the feeling she

[13]

was worth staring at. 'Now how did you know that?'

She cleared a space on the sofa and sat on it. 'Because I've actually seen you there. One of my best friends, Madge Leeds, works there—'

'Oh—yes—of course—'

'Don't interrupt,' she told him sharply. 'She says you're half-plastered most of the time but you're rather sweet. I say you may be half-plastered—probably are now—but you're not sweet—you're a stinker—'

'Well, I've sometimes wondered—'

She continued severely. 'If I'd been a man you wouldn't have talked that rubbish to me. But just because I'm a woman—'

'You shut up, this time. Miss Rapley, if you'd been a male sociologist and not an attractive girl, I'd have told you to clear out and take your idiotic research somewhere else.' Then, having asserted himself, he offered her a smile. 'But I'm sorry you didn't appreciate J. Carlton Mistletoe—an inspiration I thought. Now stop being so aggressive and Women's Libby—have a drink —'

'I'd be ashamed of myself accepting a drink from you, Dekker.'

'Good, Rapley! What will you have?'

'Not gin. Whisky perhaps.'

'Doubt if I have any. Let's see.' He went to his drinks cupboard where there was plenty of gin but not much of anything else. 'Look,' he said, turning, 'there's a drop of Cointreau here—God knows why—what about that?'

'Yes, please! Lovely! Too expensive for me but I used to drink it with my rich Aunt Sybil.'

Feeling a bit shaky he poured out the Cointreau and

some gin for himself slowly and very carefully; so they went on talking.

'Madge Leeds says you're divorced. Is that right?'

'Quite right,' he told her, pretending not to be surprised by this piece of cheek. But well—so what? 'It didn't work. We'd tried everything—except liking each other. And that we couldn't manage.' All right then—cheeky! 'What about you? Married? Living with boy friend? What?'

'Why don't you call me Kate? Also divorced. I was too young then—and *very silly*. We also found we didn't like each other.'

'You have to like each other. Love—possibly. Like certainly.' He came across with her Cointreau. 'How and where do you live now you aren't so young and silly?'

After thanking him for the Cointreau: 'I share half a house with two other girls in North Green—distant suburb. Know it?'

'No, Kate. I hardly know anywhere except Westminster and West Kensington. Do you do anything except trot around for your Community Research Thing?'

'What I'm really trying to do is to write plays.'

Dekker looked and sounded dubious. 'Is that a good idea?'

'Probably not, but it's what I want to do. Well—*cheers!*'

After his *Salut!* Dekker took a first good long look at her. She had brown hair, smooth and very clean; long eyes, greenish, brownish—anyhow, not round, prominent, pale blue, his non-favourites; a mouth in which an obstinate upper lip was probably at war with a ripe rich lower lip; and those slight hollows beneath the cheekbones that he always fancied. Certainly a wench worth looking at, though probably maddening.

'Nice drink,' she said, after calmly allowing him his long look, almost as if he were painting her portrait. 'For a stinker you're not doing too badly.'

He shrugged away this enormous condescension. 'Oh —we have our moments—we squalid stinkers.'

'With Madge Leeds?'

'Don't go female on me,' he told her rather sharply. 'Not with Madge Leeds nor with any other girl in the department. I'm a ginpot not a sexpot.'

'So I've heard.' And no smile. She got up. 'Well, thank you for my nice drink. And Goodnight—J. Carlton Mistletoe—'

'Not going already?'

In the doorway, not even turning, just over her shoulder: 'I've gone.'

She had too, no nonsense. Dekker pulled a face in her general direction, took a swig of gin, then settled down to his Alfred Brendel record of Mozart's piano concerto K.453.

Four

TWO DAYS LATER he was in Ivybridge's office again, both of them standing, chummy across the desk.

'So—thanks to Dr Belham,' said Ivybridge, 'we're giving you six weeks leave. What will you do with yourself, Dekker?'

'Nothing, probably.'

'Why not some travel—go abroad—um?'

'You forget. I told you I can't afford it—'

'So you did. Some nonsense about dry martinis. But that's asking for trouble. Demand them—or whisky—and you're on a tycoon level. Plenty of choice lower down. I know. I was over in France in April—with my wife.'

'I haven't a woman. And they enjoy it all so much more than we do.'

'Either they do—or they decide to hate it from the very start. You ought to find a girl—plenty about. Anyhow, Dekker, don't drink too much.'

'No, no,' he said, smiling. 'About the same amount.

And thanks, Ivybridge, you've been very civil about all this.'

In her tiny office next door, Madge Leeds was on the telephone but contrived to give Dekker a welcoming smile. 'I'll give Mr Ivybridge your message,' she told the phone severely, 'but I think you'll find it won't be possible before Tuesday.' Then back to human life, she cried, 'Six weeks leave—lucky you! Where are you going?'

'Everybody asks that. I'm not going anywhere.'

'But you have to do *something*—'

'I'll probably stay in bed till lunchtime—'

'Oh—you're *hopeless*—'

'I've heard that fairly often too, Madge. But sometimes it seems to me I'm less hopeless than more than half the people I know.'

She gave him a wondering look. 'In a way that's true, though it oughtn't to be, the way you behave. I saw Kate yesterday—Kate Rapley. You gave her a drink after she'd called you a stinker—right?'

'Right. She downed the drink and then walked straight out on me. Very abrupt girl, I'd say.'

'Go on.' She laughed at this example of male innocence. 'That's an old trick. We've all worked it. If you ask me, Kate's after you—'

'None of that female predator stuff—'

'She was cross-questioning me about you, though of course I couldn't tell her very much. But I did mention that horrible little pub you seem to like—'

'Only because it's so awful it's the only pub round here that isn't packed out at lunchtime. Certainly it's a terrible place, but a man can have a quiet drink and a sandwich there. It's people themselves now who represent the worst drawback. And when you consider that,' he went on, ready to be expansive.

But Madge refused to encourage him, her friend Kate offering a far more fascinating and fruitful topic. 'Do you fancy Kate?'

'I don't know, Madge.' Dekker took his time. 'I honestly don't know. I've been out of the girl-fancying game so long. She certainly answers well to a good stare.'

'She told me that too—the long look—'

'You two make Dr Belham seem like a bad-tempered amateur—'

But Madge was not to be put off. 'I'm very fond of Kate. She's a sweet girl and quite intelligent, though not as clever as she thinks she is. One minute she's sophisticated and the next minute really rather naive—'

'Aren't we all?'

'No, and don't stop me. She's had a funny history. She lost both her parents and was then passed round among a lot of aunts. To get out of that, she made a silly marriage that didn't work at all. She always knew what he was going to say next—he was that kind of man— and I think she finds you fascinating because she hasn't a clue what you'll say or do next—and though she wouldn't admit it, not until she's nailed you, she knows you're far cleverer than she is. No, don't interrupt—let me finish. But she can be a very determined girl—quite obstinate once she makes up her mind—'

'That's enough, Madge. You're beginning to make me feel like a mouse that is having a cat explained to it.' Now the phone buzzed away at her, so off he went, going along to his own office and then arranging for some of his work to be divided among several of his colleagues. An hour later he was on his way, at a six-weeks-leave leisurely pace, to that 'horrible little pub' which Madge had mentioned.

Apparently anxious not to attract any attention, it was down a side-street. At some moment of idiocy, back in the 1880s, it had been called The Carver's Arms. There was no Saloon or Public Bar nonsense about it. There was only the one longish room, about as cosy as a bankrupt warehouse. The single entrance was at the far end, away from the bar, and opposite was a frosted doorway faintly labelled GENTS. (The few women who went there would have to answer any call of nature elsewhere.) The walls, a muddy brown, were decorated by a very large mirror, spotty and sad, and a number of faded advertisements of forgotten beers and long-lost liquors. No brewery seemed to own the place and Dekker had never seen anybody who might have been the proprietor. There was only George, the barman, who had very little forehead, sunken eyes and a lot of jaw, and suggested a militant shopsteward without a union. At one end of the bar, to the left for the patrons, was a glass affair that offered shelves of ham sandwiches (not bad), dubious sausage rolls and small defeated pork pies. There were of course never many people there, and Dekker never remembered seeing anybody sitting at one of the three little tables down the room.

After George had brought the large gin and the two sandwiches Dekker had ordered, to be companionable he said, 'Heard the news this morning?'

'No,' said Dekker.

'Worse than ever.' And George turned away to attend to a double whisky and a bottle of stout.

Left to himself, Dekker did some brooding: he found this a good place for a brood. Without being anxious or even curious about the latest bad news, he wondered, not for the first time, how the politicians, including his own ass of a Minister, had the brass impudence to show their faces and harangue the public, after making such a hash of the nation's affairs. Would anybody have done any worse? Anybody? The staff of the Birkden Girls' Grammar School, say? The Barnsley Pigeon-Fanciers' Association? Selected tenants from Acacia Avenue, N.W.4? Anybody, Anybody?

'Good morning, Dekker.'

He turned to discover Miss Kate Rapley, almost at his elbow. So she could appear as unexpectedly as she could disappear. This time she was wearing some kind of thin grey suit and looked trim and very attractive. As soon as she had caught his attention, she began to look around with obvious disgust. 'Madge told me this is a horrible little pub—and it is.'

'Undoubtedly,' he replied.

'Then why come here?'

'Do you really want to know or are you just making conversation?'

'Both. Surely there must be some better pubs round here, Dekker?'

'There are, Kate. And they're all crammed with people at this time of day. Here a man can do some quiet serious drinking—and even manage a few thoughts. Would you like to know what I was thinking just before you popped up?'

'Not now—some other time. I'm hungry. When you're living with other girls, you never have a proper breakfast.'

'What can I get you? Don't touch the sausage rolls—and I'd be careful with the pies.'

'You must be mean, Dekker. Otherwise you'd take me out of here and give me a real lunch.'

'Among expense accounts fighting for tables. If you didn't hate it, you'd sadly disappoint me, Kate. I'll buy you a lager and two ham sandwiches. And not because I'm mean. It's the best I can do for you here, and I'm not going anywhere else. George!'

She nodded and even smiled, but then, looking round again, put on her disgusted face, something most young women find very easy to do. 'I suppose you spend most of your money on gin.' This came from a great height, perhaps more sociological than personal.

'A fair amount of it—yes. But on books and records too. I save on food, not going to restaurants, living chiefly on sandwiches and slabs of veal-and-ham pie.'

She gave him a frown, rather pretty really. 'A badly balanced diet, Dekker.'

'I eat the parsley. And occasional scraps of lettuce. Some fruit now and then. But never grapefruit. It belongs to the world of plastics and gross national products.'

This brought him a long wondering look. 'I don't know if I'm listening to Tom Dekker or J. Carlton Mistletoe,' she concluded, before starting to eat and drink. 'Or whether you're rather sweet and funny or might be just maddening.'

He decided against any reply to this, which did not

invite any witty ripostes.

After a few moments. 'I've turned in my sociological job,' she said. 'I can't take any more of Community Research and S. K. Overton-Briggs—'

'Who's he?'

'The Secretary—and probably J. Carlton Mistletoe's cousin, only much duller.'

'He's not S. K. Overton-Briggs all the time, is he?'

'Most of the time. And never Briggs.'

'It's a type. What are you going to do now, then, Kate? Or do you prefer Rapley?'

'No, I don't. I'm going to stay in the country and try to finish my play.'

'Is that a good idea? There are so many plays now. They do 'em—God save us!—even at lunchtime.'

'Thanks for the enthusiasm, Dekker. You've been given six weeks leave, I hear. What'll you do with that?'

'Not get dressed till noon, listening to Mozart Piano Concertos. Saunter down to a West Kensington pub—better than this—'

'In short, just go on quietly soaking,' she told him severely. 'By the way, are you sleeping with the two ballet girls at your place?'

'Never laid a finger on 'em. They're nice kids—but tedious—all exercises and chatter about the ballet.'

'Good!' Then she looked apologetic. 'Sorry! But I'm still hungry.'

'Why not? George,' he called, 'two ham sandwiches—and another large gin for me.' He thought for a moment. 'To prove I'm not mean, I'll take you out to dinner tonight—if you're free—'

'I could be,' she said promptly.

[23]

'All right then?'

'Many thanks. It was going to be our second night of shepherds' pie and beans. But I don't insist on French food—Italian will do.'

'It used to be rather good. Well now—hang on— yes, there's a place not far from here some of our fellows in the Department patronize. Forgotten the name, but I know where it is. Suppose you meet me here about half-past seven for a short drink, then we go along there. All right?'

The long eyes lighting up: 'Lovely!'

Five

IT WAS NOT lovely. Within five minutes they knew they would be lucky if this restaurant were even tolerable. Though it was now eight o'clock the place was almost empty—a bad sign. If there was a head-waiter, he must be taking the evening off. There was little or no suggestion of a real Italian restaurant. It was foreign all right but might have been dreamt up in that Eastern Mediterranean island which had been partly destroyed by an earthquake. The waiter who took sulky charge of them probably came from that same island, to which he would return at once as soon as he had had a free operation for hernia. Meanwhile he seemed to have learnt about thirty words of English, delivering them in a thick sullen tone.

When Kate, who had already despaired of the place, pointed to something on the menu, he said, 'No, no. Is off today. No good.'

Dekker had a try. 'What about this?' he asked, pointing.

'No good. Off. *Off.*' And the waiter stepped back and

seemed to be staring at the three posters of young women with enormous breasts who were advertising obscure Mediterranean resorts.

Dekker looked hard in his direction. 'We're not boring you, are we?' The waiter made no reply, clearly not understanding what had been said to him. 'Well, Kate, what about melon first, then macaroni or spaghetti? Okay? *Bolognaise* or *milanaise*?'

The waiter was with him now. 'All the same here. One kind only—'

'What—with an Italian chef?—'

'No Italian chef here. Two chefs. One Pakistani. One Turk. Tonight is Turk.'

For the next hour they sat in a disaster area, making faces at each other. The food was no good, not even the melon; the wine must have come from that same earthquake island; and the waiter became more aggressive, banging everything down, and clumsier and clumsier, knocking over the wine bottle that Dekker just rescued in time, and contriving to spill sauce on Kate's dress so that she all but spat at him. Over the coffee, which at least was tolerable, Dekker began to apologize.

'Don't,' Kate told him. 'It wasn't your fault.'

'I oughtn't to have risked it. But now you see what I mean. Too bad to drink gin in ugly little pubs! But it just keeps me floating along still in my right mind, with so much of everything either terrible or idiotic. I haven't done much travelling lately, but would a place like this be tolerated in Paris or Rome or Vienna, in Germany, Holland or Sweden? No, only in London, England, probably under the patronage of the T.U.C. No doubt there's some trace of quality left here, but can we afford it? Or am I still being mean?'

When the waiter put down the bill aggressively, Dekker paid it and carefully added a tip. The waiter accepted it without a word and began to move away. Dekker called him back. 'Just to thank you,' he began smoothly, 'for accepting my tip—gratuity—*pourboire*— *Trinkgeld*—for your excellent service.' But the waiter only stared, shrugged, went away.

'Well, if he didn't enjoy that, I did, Tom Dekker,' said Kate smiling. 'Gosh—what a waiter! I think he spilt everything except the money. But—now what? And it's important because I must have a serious talk with you.'

'Then, if you don't mind, it's back to my ugly pub. We can have a quiet drink there, and I'll try to be just as serious as you, Kate.'

Ten minutes later he was wagging a finger at George. 'Yes, gin for me—and if you've a touch of that old Armagnac left for Miss Rapley, I think she'd enjoy it.'

'Can do, Mr Dekker.'

It was as quiet as usual, but even so, while George. went to find his old Armagnac, a middle-aged drunk came reeling up. He had a gaping mouth and looked not unlike a purple carp in neat Terylene.

'Seen you before,' he said to Dekker, 'but can't place the lil' lady.' He pointed and goggled away. 'Like to place the lil' lady.'

'I'm not little,' said Kate, 'and I'd like you to go away and stay there.'

'Now tha's rude—*rude*—'

Looking solemn, Dekker tapped him on the shoulder. 'I've a message for you from Charlie—'

'Wha'? Good ol' Charlie!'

'He was in here,' said Dekker, still solemn, 'looking for you. And he asked me to tell you he's gone across to the Crown—saloon bar—expecting you—'

'Jolly good,' said the drunk. 'An' thanks a lot of a lot.' And at once went staggering away.

'Thank goodness for that!' said Kate. 'Do you know him, Tom?'

'Never set eyes on him before. But his type always has a drinking pal called Charlie. And he won't come back.'

She didn't even give him a smile. 'Oh—you're so infuriating, Tom! You can be so quick and clever—and yet—and yet—' And she shook her head.

George was back with the drinks. 'Thanks, George. Pay you later.' Dekker picked up the drinks and then looked rather hard at Kate. 'Now then, girl, what's all this about?'

'Wait a minute. Is there any reason why we shouldn't sit at one of those tables?'

'I've never seen it done yet, but there can't be any rule against it. Choose one.'

The table seemed to be covered with ancient oilcloth. The chairs were equally old, and small and rickety, not bad for a serious discussion but ready to discourage any lolling and idle badinage. 'You'll dam' well have to attend to what I say here, Dekker. No J. Carlton Mistletoe stuff at this table, buster.' However, she tried her Armagnac. 'What a heavenly drink! I nearly asked for more Cointreau, but now I'm glad I didn't.'

'I've never understood what it's *doing* here,' he told her. 'George never ordered it. Before his time.'

He said no more because he felt she wanted to say

someting to him but didn't know yet how to begin. Finally, it came.

'Tom—I'm now going to challenge you.'

'Not a good idea, Kate. There are some men who can't refuse a challenge. But I can—easily—'

'I know—and that's just it. No—listen, Tom—this is serious. Tomorrow I go down into the country to work on my play. Nobody knows where I'm going—except one person. And I'll only tell you this: I'm not leaving England. And that's all. If you want to see any more of me, you'll have to find me. If you do find me, I promise you a beautiful welcome. If you don't, if you just go soaking and sozzling around, you'll never see me again.'

'That's too tough. You don't mean it.'

'I do. I like you, Tom, like you quite a lot already, but I can't afford to invest my emotion in another dead loss of a man. Either find me—or fade out. I mean it.'

'I can see you do,' said Dekker. 'Your hands are trembling—'

She pulled her hands out of sight at once. 'They're not. Shut up!' She waited a moment. 'Well, what do you say?'

He held up a forefinger and there was something departmental about his manner. 'We must consider this challenge of yours, Kate. You disappear into the country. I must stop sitting around, idly boozing, and find you. If I don't, then we shan't meet again. But if our roles were reversed, would you accept such a challenge?'

'Certainly not,' she replied without any hesitation.

'Well, there you are!'

'No, you've missed the point, Tom. I believe that if you stopped sitting around and lapping up gin and really made up your mind to find me, you're clever enough to do it. Don't ask me how, that's up to you.'

'Your friend Madge warned me you could be very obstinate—but this is a bit much. Tomorrow you turn yourself into a needle going into a haystack, and unless I'm astonishingly clever—or lucky—we don't meet again. And all this just as I've begun thinking about you.'

'Have you?' Though she didn't mean it to slip out like that—all eager. To cover any confusion, she finished her Armagnac.

'That's all you get, Kate.' He turned himself into a grim smiler—not easy. 'No pretty speeches for the vanishing girl.'

'Who's about to vanish right now.' She stood up and then looked and sounded reproachful. 'So you can't take a challenge? Too far gone perhaps?'

'Far gone perhaps,' said Dekker cheerfully, 'but I didn't refuse the challenge. We'll see—we'll see. After all, it might be one way of spending a leave.' He was now walking her to the door.

'Don't come out,' she told him. 'I'm going to rush to the Tube.' She hesitated a moment, then gave him one of those hasty pecks on the cheek. Then really hurried away.

Back with his gin at the table, Dekker told himself that hasty pecks of that sort can be interpreted in two very different ways. They pass for kisses when no real kissing is intended, among women greeting one another or facing a man who expects some demonstration and rates no more than a peck. On the other hand, at a dramatic extreme, when a girl may want to kiss a man full and lingering on the mouth but dare not risk it, she rushes into a hasty cheek job because she feels she must do something. What had been behind Kate's impulsive movement? Dekker didn't know. There was, he concluded as he went for *just one for the road*, more and more he didn't know.

Six

THE FOLLOWING AFTERNOON, sunny, warm, Kate was staring dreamily at a landscape in which hills were a blue haze and woods flashed up and then melted away. She was on the road, sitting next to the driver of the foreign and obviously very expensive sports car, a talkative woman, very smart and still handsome, though in her early sixties. She was talking about the house towards which they were moving at an even 55 miles an hour.

'But I refused to take it beyond October, though. After that it's murder in England.'

Even Kate's objection was slow and dreamy. 'It isn't, you know. Sometimes in a fine November it's heavenly. There can be the most marvellous colouring and misty effects.'

'There can also be rain for ever. I know, child. However, I think you'll love this house. Oldish without being inconveniently ancient. Not too big, but not poky—just right for us, plus anybody else who turns up. Quiet room for you to work in—you *are* going to do some writing, aren't you, my dear?'

'Yes, I told you. On my play. A witty comedy, I hope, when I get round to feeling witty, not easy when you're by yourself staring at a blank sheet of typing paper. Perhaps the garden will help.'

'It might. It's a sweet little garden,' the older woman continued, 'bliss after those pompous boring château things I've had to endure. I've got a woman who's supposed to be a reliable plain cook. Probably means stodge. But I'll have some *Cordon Bleu* treats sent down from London.' She stopped for a little appreciation, but Kate said nothing. 'Are you listening, my dear, or are you trying to work out your play?'

'Oh—no, not yet.'

'Then you're worrying about a man—'

'You're too clever—'

'I'm not that clever but I've had a hell of a lot of experience, my dear. So it's a man.'

'Yes,' said Kate. 'I was with him last night, and now I'm wondering if I didn't say the wrong thing to him or say it in the wrong way—'

'My dear, the number of times I've worried about that! *Men*! And don't tell me you've found another tailors' dummy like that one you married—what was his name?'

'Derek. No, this one's just the opposite. I never know what he's going to say or do. I told him I was disappearing and challenged him to sober up and find me—'

'Well, that's something I never tried. Look—tell me all about it when I've stopped being responsible for this

[33]

car. We'd be wasting our talk on these corkscrew roads. As soon as we're having our first drink in the house, we'll try to decide if you've been very clever or behaved like an idiot . . .'

Seven

WHILE KATE WAS moving away from him at nearly a mile a minute, Dekker was in Madge Leeds' little office. She was as anxious as he was—perhaps even more anxious—to discuss the dramatic Kate development, but it was a busy afternoon, with her phone buzzing away. She had just told it, with some severity, that she didn't know and couldn't be expected to know.

'All she'd tell me,' she said to Dekker, returning to real life, 'was that she was going to stay in the country and write her play. We're supposed to be close friends but that's all she'd tell me. Thought if I knew anything I'd pass it on to you.'

'And wouldn't you, Madge?'

'Not at first—after a week perhaps.' The phone called her. 'Extension 14—Mr Ivybridge. . . . No, you want Extension 24. . . . Yes, I'm *sure*.' She turned to Dekker. 'She's trying to reform you, of course. I think it's a dotty idea, and really hard on poor you—that is, if you've fallen for her—'

'Well, no, I wouldn't go as far as that—'

'I would. If you hadn't, you'd have told her what to do with her daft challenge. Whereas, here you are, asking me to give you the smallest possible clue.' But the phone claimed her again: 'Yes, Mr Ivybridge is expecting him at five. And whatever you've been told, Mrs Sands, that's definite—five without fail.'

Dekker had now sat down on a chair too small for him, and had brought out a note book. He then glared at the telephone, which was claiming Madge once more. 'No, he won't be back until five,' she told it, 'and then he's got somebody coming. . . . Well, don't blame me.'

'Madge,' he began as she turned to him, 'be a good sweet girl and switch off that phone for a couple of minutes. The point is,' he continued as soon as she had done this, 'we must be systematic. There are obviously two early approaches. One impersonal, the other personal. Now whatever Kate may have told us, there may be people with whom she's left her new address just because they may have something important to say to her. And I feel I'd rather try them first before making it personal, trying aunts and so forth. For example, she might have given her new address to her former employers, who might owe her some money—'

'Well,' said Madge, 'that's the Community Research Social Science Council, somewhere in Bloomsbury. It's run by a man called S. K. Overton-Briggs. Kate couldn't *bear* him.'

'I don't like the sound of him,' said Dekker. 'Anyway, we'll see. Anything else?'

'Yes, there's the North Green Drama Club—'

Dekker shook his head. 'That seems a pity. Why?'

'Kate's a member and wrote a play for them once. I saw it.'

'Any good?'

'A bit of a mess, I thought,' said Madge. 'But she might easily be keeping in touch. So try the North Green Drama Club—only two minutes from the Tube Station up there. Look—I'll have to switch the phone back on again in a second—'

'Hold it! Hold it! Relatives?'

But he was too late. She was back on the phone: 'I've told you already—you want Extension 24. And this is still 14. . . . Well I ought to know, oughtn't I?' Ringing off, she muttered, 'That girl's a complete idiot.'

'There are more and more of 'em,' said Dekker. 'Now —about relatives. You feel Kate may be staying with an aunt?'

'Yes. She hates hotels and anyhow I know she's too hard up. She has four aunts, but only one lives in London. We went to see her once—a kind of veteran Women's Libber—tough and ancient. Mildred Dragby's her name—Mrs Dragby, though you'd think she'd be against taking a husband's name, wouldn't you?'

'No, I just wouldn't know. Is she in the telephone book?'

'She was.' But the phone buzzed at her again. While she was answering it, Dekker examined the notes he had made. Three definite lines of enquiry. One of them ought to give him the clue he needed. He felt an optimistic businesslike fellow for once. Wishing to thank Madge he waited until she had stopped wrestling over the phone with a noisy Central European, a Dr Fewglemann or

something. Then he patted her on the shoulder, forget-
ting that girls nearly always consider this detestable.
'Thank you and bless you, my child,' he said, turning
himself now into an old hermit. 'Blessings on you!'

Eight

IT WAS NEXT morning when Dekker found his way to the Community Research Social Science Council's offices. No researchers were arriving and departing. Either the Council started work very early in the morning or its grant was running out. There was a girl typing in a corridor. He told her he wished to see Mr S. K. Overton-Briggs on a personal matter. She went clickclacking to the end of the corridor, turned to the left, but was back in a few moments, suggesting he should sit down.

She was a short, dark girl with angry eyes. 'He's sitting there, not doing a dam' thing, but he'll keep you waiting—you'll see.'

'Like that, is he?'

'With knobs on.'

'Tell me,' said Dekker smiling, 'did you know Kate Rapley here?'

'Yes, though she was on the outside most of the time. Rather tall, goodlooking, bit snooty. But snooty all round, not just to me, which made it better. She and Mastermind along there didn't get on at all—one up for her. Your girl friend?'

'Not exactly. But she's vanished—and I'm trying to find her. She didn't leave an address with you, by any chance, did she?'

'No, she didn't. But Briggs may have it.'

'In confidence now,' said Dekker. 'What would happen if he heard you saying *Briggs* and not S. K. Overton-Briggs?'

'I'd be out—treading water again in a typing pool.' After a short silence, a black box on her table came to life in a disagreeable fashion, and issued a command to her. Obviously it could listen too, for she said, 'Mr S. K. Overton-Briggs is free to see you, Mr Dekker. This way, please.'

It was quite a large room. The chap was sitting behind his desk and didn't rise when Dekker entered, to observe with distaste the fish eye, the long nose, the close tiny mouth. However, Dekker began heartily, 'Good morning, Mr S. K. Overton-Briggs!' This brought him only the ghost of a nod. 'I'm wondering if you could do me a small personal favour. Could you?'

'I've no idea.' No smile, no anything.

With all his civil service experience, Dekker realised in a flash the type he was now facing. He knew all about this zombie technique. There would be the blank face, no encouraging little noises to ease the situation, not a drop of oil for the machinery of talk. But he would try to do his best. 'No idea? No, of course not. Stupid of me. Well, the point is—I'm trying to get the new address of one of your researchers—'

[40]

'It is not the policy of the Council to do this.'

Dekker glanced at the wall to his right, chiefly in order to keep his temper. It seemed to be decorated with a milk-chocolate wallpaper and some late and horrible throw-outs of the Abstract Movement. No help at all there. 'I can well understand that, Mr S. K. Overton-Briggs, but this particular researcher, Kate Rapley, is no longer with your Council.'

'Quite true,' said Briggs, almost bursting into conversation. 'So where she is now is no concern of ours.'

In the short silence that followed, Dekker lost his temper. 'But—dam' it all, man, you might have to forward letters or a cheque or something, so she must have left you some address.'

Briggs, as Dekker thought of him now, waited about ten seconds just to increase the misery, then said, 'She didn't.'

'Mr S. K. Overton-Briggs,' Dekker began with angry deliberation and over-emphasis, 'this has nothing to do with your Research Council. As I told you at first, I'm merely asking you for a small personal favour. You may have heard of small personal favours—there are still a few around. And this girl happens to be a close friend—' And he stopped there.

Another pause. 'Indeed!'

'Yes, indeed,' Dekker replied warmly. 'A close friend —and likely soon—to be much closer—'

Briggs now came to life, but of course in a nasty suspicious sneering fashion. 'Then why hasn't she given you her new address?' Short interval here, though no reply expected. 'You know what I think?'

'No,' said Dekker, 'and I've been trying to imagine.'

[41]

'Fishy.' This was delivered from the cod's-eye-and-long-nose bench with some complacency. 'Distinctly fishy.'

'Fishy?' Was this what Dekker had heard?

'My verdict—absolutely fishy.'

'My God!' cried Dekker. 'It's like being told by a fish you're fishy. Kate Rapley has a good sensible—if slightly daft—warm human reason why she's not told me where she's gone. But I'm not trying to pop anything else into this deep freeze.' He held the door open so that the secretary might overhear him. 'Goodbye, Briggs!'

She must have heard him because she squeezed his arm and said, 'I'll have to be careful for the rest of the day, because S. K. Overton will be so upset, but I wouldn't have missed that for anything. Don't forget to tell Kate Rapley when you find her. You can also tell her from me she's lucky.'

The Carvers' had an old wall telephone that the G.P.O. must have long overlooked, years and years before it had started overlooking almost everything. Having swallowed half a large gin, Dekker used this instrument to give his news to Madge Leeds. (But first getting Extension 24 instead of 14) 'No, no, a complete washout. I think Briggs transferred his dislike of Kate to me. However, I was able to make a point or two . . . I'll visit the North Green Drama Club this evening. Not far from the Underground, you said, didn't you? . . . . I always feel a little disturbed, not quite in touch with reality, after a long journey in the Underground, but no doubt it'll wear off . . .'

Nine

DEKKER FELT HE had been so long down there, joggling away facing two evening papers without ever catching a glimpse of their readers, that he half-expected to find himself, surfacing at last, in some utterly strange place, perhaps a North Green with a scattering of igloos and seal-hunters. But it looked like anywhere else in London, with stores asking you to buy something to save money, an appeal that always mystified Dekker. After lingering outside a record shop for a minute or two, he crossed the road and finally discovered the Drama Club squashed between a delicatessen and a dry cleaner's. A tiny entrance hall was largely filled and completely dominated by a plump middle-aged woman, a pouter-pigeon type and probably bossy, who had a cigarette smouldering away in a long ivory holder.

Though he knew it must be, Dekker began with 'This *is* the North Green Drama Club, isn't it?'

'Yes it is,' she replied rather haughtily, 'but I don't think you're a member, are you?'

[43]

'No, I'm not. But I wanted—'

She cut him short. 'And we're busy rehearsing our new production—with the North Green Shiners—

But Dekker could do some short-cutting. 'Oh—what are they?'

'Well—really! The Shiners are the best-known Pop Group in North London—easily the best-known—and quite rightly so. And I really can't have anybody disturbed. If you're calling about lighting or costume hire, you must choose some other time. This is a very important first run-through. So—Goodnight!'

Dekker was now even haughtier than she was. 'Oh—come—come—this won't do. It really won't, you know.'

'Why won't it?' A doubt creeping in there, perhaps.

'I must point out that I'm J. Carlton Mistletoe—of the drama department of the Arts Council, from which you've been asking a grant—'

A flustered pouter-pigeon now. 'Oh—I'm sorry—I didn't realize—'

'Obviously. This way, is it? Thank you.'

They were rehearsing in a broad but rather shallow room with a wide bare platform to his left as he entered. Obviously it could be turned into a theatre of sorts when they were ready to perform. Now there were only a few scattered kitchen chairs on which two or three people were perched. He could hardly see them because the only light, naked and harsh, was above the platform-stage. Here, busy at rehearsal, were two young women, amateur actresses, and a middle-aged worried director and a middle-aged stage-manager who looked so alike they might have been twins, uncles perhaps to Tweedle-dee and Tweedledum. And then, not without a shudder, he saw that spread along the back of the stage were the North Green Shiners, all six of them, together with a lot of glittering equipment. They themselves, he discovered, were in costume and tremendously made-up, but their shiny green costumes and faces being largely in shadow, they might have been patients in a jungle fever hospital. At the moment they were as quiet as so many verdant mice, but Dekker couldn't help feeling they were already on the alert—waiting to deafen him.

Harshly revealed by the rehearsal light were the two young women, one in clashing 'separates' and the other with a big bottom in defeated trousers. They were doing a quarrel scene out of a social level rather lower than their own.

'An' just let me tell you something now, Maggie,' Trousers shouted.

'You couldn't tell me nothing, dearie,' snarled Separates, overdoing it.

'Well, what about this then. Jerry an' me have bin living together for the last three months—'

'An' just doing it for laughs, he told me—'

'And that's a bloody lie, for a start.' Both overdoing it now.

As they glared at each other in silence, Dekker approached a young man standing near him. 'Sorry to bother you, but I wonder if you could tell me—'

'Jerry's on now, Eric,' the stage-manager shouted.

Jerry-Eric, an athletic type, leapt on to the platform, where the two young women greeted his appearance with smiles of relief that were clean out of character.

'You've no cue here, Eric,' said the director. 'You go straight into *You chicks*—'

'Sorry, Stanley.' He started, acting his head off. 'You chicks,' he bellowed, 'look as if you're going to do some pecking and scratching—'

'Listen to you, Jerry!' cried Trousers.

'That ought to come later, Muriel,' said the director. 'But never mind. Leave it for now. Carry on, Eric.'

As Eric hesitated, the stage-manager prompted him. *'Now break it up—'*

'Now break it up while I give you some big big news—'

'Hold it, Eric. You'll really have to project there—with the big big news—'

'While I give you some big big news,' said Eric repeating himself exactly.

Snarler Separates had her cue here. 'Here we go again —God's gift—the Wonder Boy—'

'Just bloody jealous, that's all,' Trousers told her, all acting of course. 'What is it, Jerry?'

Eric was sure of this line and brought it out triumphantly. *'I'm going to join the Shiners.'*

Mistaking this for their cue, which it wasn't, the Shiners went into action at once. The noise was bad enough during the first minute but then, when two enormous loud speakers had been switched on, it was appalling, not so much a din as a pain in the ears. The director and the stage-manager were probably shouting their heads off but of course they couldn't be heard and looked as if they were dancing in front of the Shiners. All three players were waving their arms as if they were not remonstrating with the Shiners but conducting them. Ear-splitting chaos had arrived, and Dekker wondered whether to get out while he was still in his right mind.

[46]

However, when the Shiners had been persuaded to keep quiet and the director and the stage-manager were trying to sort out their cues, Dekker noticed an elderly woman sitting a few yards away.

'Excuse me,' said Dekker, 'but are you a member of this club?'

'Oldest but one,' she told him proudly. 'I'm playing Maggie's mother in this piece.'

'Splendid! Well, now I wonder if you could tell me—'

But the director had turned to shout at him. 'Quiet there! Keep it quiet. It's bad enough without a lot of chat out there.' He swung round to the Shiner leader, a very hairy type who had come forward into the light, and with his shiny green make-up and costume now looked like a ruined vegetable.

'All right,' said the director, 'if you must come in to-night—and remember I was against it when we still have to go through these intimate scenes—for God's sake do it on the right cue.'

'You'll get it from Jerry—Eric here,' said the stage-manager. 'Give it to 'em, Eric old man.'

'Okay.' And he gave it to them, loud and clear. 'So we're playing next week in Sudbury.'

Nothing happened. The Shiners might have been vegetables in a hard winter.

Eric tried again, even louder and clearer. 'So we're playing next week in Sudbury.'

'Like hell we are,' cried a Shiner. 'Man, you're giving me bad vibes.'

The director lost the little bit of temper he had left. 'That's your cue,' he told them angrily. 'That's where you first come in. How d'you mean you haven't got it? You must have it—'

Dekker tried the elderly woman again. 'I must explain that I'm enquiring about a girl I know called Kate Rapley—'

'Just a minute,' she said, 'I don't want to miss this. Always enjoy these dust-ups at rehearsal.' And she cackled away.

'Don't be so bloody thick.' The director was loud and angry. 'We're not saying you're on next week at Sudbury. That's a line in the play—and why haven't they had it?' he asked the stage-manager.

'They have, Stanley. All I had to give 'em. Out of their depth. I did warn you right at the start. All right, Eric—just once more—'

'So we're playing next week in Sudbury.'

It was worse than before, a kind of aural brainstorm. Only the elderly woman, who seemed to be beating time, could endure it. All the others scrambled off the platform and were mouthing speeches at one another. Dekker couldn't take any more. He might be screaming soon. He crept back into the little entrance hall.

'Find it a bit noisy, do you?' the woman asked, with a bright smile for the Arts Council.

There is such a thing as an affirmative groan, and Dekker produced one for her.

'It's a new experimental piece we're doing—a mixture of human drama in the East End and Pop music. It's called *All Goes Pop*. Clever, eh?'

'Descriptive certainly—'

'It's written by a young Finn—'

'Some young thing—um?' Dekker laughed. 'I thought for a moment you said a *young Finn*—'

'I did. He came to see us on his first visit to England. Of course our director, Mr Stanley Dadd, had to help him with the East End part—'

'Mr Dadd knows the East End, does he?'

'Well, not really. He was in Cheltenham up to a year ago—'

'Anyhow,' said Dekker, babbling along with her, 'there seemed to be more than a suggestion of North Green—'

'That's right. Because we got the Shiners, you see— North Green Shiners—you heard them, didn't you?'

'I did indeed. And I'm looking forward to keeping at least quarter of a mile away from them in the future. By the way,' he continued, gazing steadily at her, 'we wanted to get in touch with a promising young playwright here —Kate Rapley.'

'Oh—her! She's left us—finish! Gone without telling us where.'

'Are you sure?' the sinking heart enquired.

'I ought to be. I'm the Secretary of the Club, aren't I? And we're not going to miss her, I can tell you. Too stuck-up for us, Kate Rapley was. We like to be chummy here.'

'And Miss Rapley wasn't chummy?'

'Never even tried.'

'I'm delighted to hear it. Goodnight.'

He returned across the road, towards the Underground station, but turned into a Lounge Bar. Ever since he had heard that reference to 'soaking and sozzling' he had been cutting down his gins, but he felt he was entitled to at least one before tunnelling his way to West Kensington. He was not a Lounge Bar type. This North

Green sample was filled with middle-aged men either with tough wives or with girls for whom they were neglecting the not-so-tough wives left at home. It was also loud with the hard mechanical laughter, essentially the wrong sort, that follows 'Stop me if you've heard this one.' The idiot scene might be said to be the Overground to the Underground about to claim him, suddenly feeling old for his years and deep in melancholy.

Ten

KATE WAS ONLY just in time for the usual cocktail
before dinner. She hadn't changed and knew she must
be looking unready, untidy, unkempt, un-everything.
Aunt Sybil, wearing another long dress, a dark red this
one, was pouring out a dry martini and smoking a
Gauloise. Though blissfully tolerant as a rule, she now
regarded Kate with some disapproval.

'I'm terribly sorry, Sybil,' said Kate, 'but I got
absolutely stuck in my second act and was getting
frantic—'

'You should have stopped earlier. I've known a
number of first-rate artists of all kinds, and almost
always they told me they knew when to stop and when
to push on. That's something you'll have to learn, my
dear.'

'Yes,' said Kate meekly. 'And there's a lot more I'll
have to learn somehow. Perhaps I ought to make it a
more dramatic comedy. Sitting up there with my type-
writer I don't feel very witty.'

'Well, I might be able to help you there,' said Sybil,
pouring out. 'I've made a vodka martini tonight and

that may make you feel rather wittier. Here. But that's
not what I meant when I said I might be able to help
you. Incidentally, the only time I show any signs of wit
is when I'm screamingly angry with men, who are
almost always too thick, flustered or pompous, to enjoy
my wit. It's wasted on them and of course I never remember what I said myself. Try these cocktail bits and
pieces. They came in a parcel from London this morning. But when you've stopped crunching I've important
news for you—'

'Not about Tom?' Kate was alight at once.

'Tom? Tom? What Tom?'

Kate had to switch herself off. 'The man I challenged
to find me, remember?'

'Oh—that wretched fellow—'

'He's not a wretched fellow—'

'If he'd had any sense he'd have grabbed hold of you
when you talked that rubbish to him. It's the only way
to deal with us when we're being silly.'

'I wasn't being silly. It was very serious. He could
waste his life, just boozing away.'

'Well, let's forget about him. Now, my dear, this'll be
the last evening you'll come down looking as if you'd
been dragged through a hedge. Why? Because I've had a
cable from Marcel—you remember my French stepson?
—saying he's coming to stay, arriving tomorrow. Isn't
that exciting?'

Kate risked a little frown. 'I don't know, Sybil. We
haven't met since we were kids. What's he like now?'

'Rather solemn—he's in films and wears a pompous
little beard—but really very attractive, very gentle and
sweet. Speaks English now, after spending about three

years in Hollywood.'

'Does he talk about films all the time?'

'Yes of course. They all do. Still that's not too bad—it might have been geology or politics.'

'What does he do in films, Sybil?'

'I never really understand, my dear. How can one when it's all so confusing? Sometimes he seems to be an assistant producer or director and sometimes he seems to be writing scripts, and at other times he seems to be doing everything at once. But anyhow it'll be a man about the place. Take your mind off your boozy civil servant, my dear.'

'No, it won't,' said Kate, not rudely but stoutly. 'I'm beginning to feel I've been too hard on him. How can he find me unless I give him a clue?'

'Kate darling, don't weaken now. Absolutely fatal to give in—especially with a man who drinks.' She filled her glass. 'I ought to know. Three husbands—one British, one French, one American—and they *all* drank too much. Rupert had whiskies and sodas all day and half the night. André never stopped—wine and brandy—and so had a liver like an old boot and a frightful temper. My American—poor old Irving—drank anything and everything all the time—from applejack down to tequila. And I tell you, my dear, don't give them an inch.'

'But how on earth can poor Tom Dekker possibly find me?'

'Let him do the worrying. You think about your play. Then listen sweetly to Marcel talking about films. Perhaps he'll ask you to help him with a script.'

'Probably all violence and raw sex now—'

'I'm against the violence, but all sex is raw—otherwise it isn't sex, just an embarrassing messing about.'

'And I've had that,' Kate muttered.

'Don't tell me. I've had everything.' She finished her martini, then looked around with some complacency. 'Not bad now, y'know, dear.'

'It's more and more *you*, Sybil. You really *are* clever, just doing it somehow with bits and pieces. Here's a room that must have been furnished and decorated by Mrs Thing for Brigadier Thing, your landlord, and now it looks part-French, part-American, already.' Having returned her aunt's smile, Kate went on: 'Of course I could always ring up Madge Leeds to ask what's happening to Tom.' And she explained about Madge Leeds.

'You couldn't make a worse move,' her aunt replied emphatically. 'Stupid from every point of view. It shows you're weakening.'

'I wouldn't tell her where I am,' Kate began.

'She might have the call traced. On the other hand, if she likes your Tom as you say she does, she might decide to hook him herself. Oh—I know—your best friend and all that, but I know what best female friends can get up to. No, no, no—let's go in to dinner—you challenged him. He seemed to accept your challenge. And if he simply goes back to the bottle, after the first few days, then he's no good to you. I fancy you need a man cleverer than you are. So wait and stick it out. It's what we women are doing half the time, anyhow. Just grilled ham and broad beans first,' she added as they entered the dining room. 'But then, from London, *fond d'artichauts . . .*'

Eleven

'SO FAR, NO good,' Dekker told Madge Leeds over the phone. 'Briggs, where she'd worked, was even blanker than I'd anticipated. He disliked Kate, he soon disliked me, and he has probably a poor opinion of our whole galaxy. The Drama Club was rehearsing a pop group and gave me earache. She never told them where she was going, just left them—being *stuck-up* in their opinion. If she'd felt at home in that club, I'd have abandoned this search. There's a snob—not social but intellectual and aesthetic—coming out in me. But now, Madge, all I'm left with is the London end of the aunts—Aunt Mildred —Mrs Dragby—and if I can't charm anything useful out of her, then I'm dished. Yes, of course I'll keep in touch . . .'

The place looked more like a very solid private house than a set of offices. But on the door he read—

WOMEN'S SOCIAL AND POLITICAL LIBERATION FRONT

Chairperson: Mildred Dragby

The door was open so he made his way into a reception room, with a secretary's desk in it but no secretary. There were some watercolour landscapes round the walls. Dekker examined them with some care, and was surprised to find they were quite good—no masterpieces of course—what a hope!—but better than anything he had ever done. The secretary came in with an apology, a black dress, white hair but a pleasant youngish face.

Dekker offered her a smile she well deserved. 'Good morning. I have an appointment with Mrs Dragby. Tom Dekker.'

'Ah—yes, of course,' she said briskly. 'At the Ministry of Export Development and Promotion, I believe.'

'Now how do you know that? I didn't say so on the telephone.'

'Mrs Dragby asked me to look you up. She's very meticulous.'

'She must be. But I'm not here from the Ministry. It's really a personal matter—'

'You can explain that, Mr Dekker. Mrs Dragby can see you now—'

'Wait a moment, please! I know about watercolours. And these are very good. I've been having a real look at them. Who did them?'

'Mr Dragby, who died about eight years ago. He was a lawyer but his hobby was painting. When I tell Mrs Dragby you're here, I'll also tell her what you said about his pictures. She'll be so pleased.'

While he waited, Dekker wondered if there were any

more, perhaps even better, in Mrs Dragby's room. But there weren't, as he noticed at once; just some engravings and photographs. It was a very solid and severe room. Mrs Dragby was sitting at a large desk. She was a massive woman, with cropped grey hair, and could have posed, at a pinch, as a sergeant in Napoleon's Old Guard. After greeting him, not without some trace of warmth, she said, 'You suggested to Miss Bancroft that you understand and appreciate watercolours.'

'I do. So well that I've stopped painting them myself —just not good enough. Your husband's are far better than mine ever were. I'm disappointed not to find any in here.'

'The truth is, Mr Dekker, I've no eye for painting, so that I never knew whether or not Robert, my husband, was wasting his time.'

'I assure you,' said Dekker warmly, 'he was not. He was well up to a good professional standard. Better, I'd say, than the usual watercolourist who gets into the Royal Academy. If you have any more at home—'

'I am at home. This is my home as well as my office. And the pictures hanging in the reception room are all I've got.' She had a deepish voice, kept at an even pitch. It was hard to tell from it if she was pleased or displeased, whatever her Miss Bancroft might say. 'Do sit down, Mr Dekker. We here at the W.S.P.L.F. don't see much of you at the M.E.D.F. We spend rather more time with the B.O.T. and the M.O.E. and of course the F.O. and the H.O.'

'You do, do you?' As a civil servant he had played this initial game for years, but too many coming all at once left him bewildered. He tried a smile. 'Sounds rather as if you're just rollicking with the alphabet.'

This was received with some severity. 'Mr Dekker, I must tell you that one reason I have been able to do so much in my chosen field—*is*—that I'm entirely deficient in a sense of humour.'

Dekker was genuinely delighted by this bold statement. Without any thought of pleasing her, he told her so. 'This country is crammed to suffocation with people who cackle and guffaw at bad jokes and congratulate themselves on having a sense of humour. When real humour was as common in England as bread and cheese, nobody was talking about this sense of humour. It was when we left the Victorians behind, we began nudging and chuckling and grinning on principle, deathly solemn at heart. Thank you, Mrs Dragby, for that sensible but most unusual confession, if you'll allow me to say so.'

'I'll also allow you to tell me why you're here, Mr Dekker.'

'It's strictly a private matter, Mrs Dragby. The Department didn't send me. Actually I'm on leave.'

'Indeed—why?'

Dekker felt that she didn't approve of civil servants being away from their duties and out of touch with the B.O.T. and the M.O.E. and the F.O. He would have to move carefully now. 'I'm supposed to be off-colour.'

If she had felled him with a left hook, he could hardly have been more surprised when he heard her reply to this. She gave him a searching look, and said, 'You are drinking too much, aren't you?'

While he gaped at her, she offered him a grim little smile.

'Don't look so astonished, Mr Dekker. There is quite a simple explanation. All government departments employ a number of women, often with access to confidential information. Among these women are members of our Movement, and they make reports to us.'

'Yes, I see. Simple—and terrifying. Perhaps I ought to explain that while I'm an old-fashioned feminist, I'm not with you Liberators. I think you're in danger of exchanging the feminine principle, which I revere, for the masculine principle. It's like a racehorse wanting to be a rhinoceros.'

'In a jungle it may be necessary to look like a rhinoceros. But why do you drink too much, Mr Dekker?'

Once again, Dekker explained his 'floating' theory, which made little impression on Mrs Dragby, not one to do any floating. He ended by describing quite frankly Kate's challenge. 'And now she's disappeared into the country somewhere, though still in England—she told me that much.'

'Partly a girlish attempt to reform you,' said Mrs Dragby. 'But for what other purpose?'

'She wants to finish a play she's writing.'

'I'm sorry to hear it. Katherine did well at school and college. Then concentrated on the social sciences, but then developed what seemed to me a frivolous interest in the Theatre. I don't despise the Theatre, Mr Dekker. Ibsen and Shaw, for example, concentrated attention on woman's plight. But most plays seem to me idle nonsense, and this is what I fear Katherine wishes to write. Are you trying to encourage this, Mr Dekker?'

'Not at all. I don't particularly like the Theatre—

hardly ever go. But then I don't like the social sciences either.'

'What *do* you like?'

'I like your niece, Kate.'

'As a sexual object?'

'As a person who might also be a desirable sexual object.'

'Not a bad answer.' She thought for a moment, then astonished him all over again. 'What is it you drink too much of, Mr Dekker? Oh—gin?' She rang for the secretary. 'Miss Bancroft, if we have any gin, bring some for Mr Dekker. And I'll take a glass of the dry sherry.'

'Mrs Dragby,' he began warmly, 'one reason why I try to keep floating along is that now hardly anybody surprises me. It's all like the news being flogged to death by the media. But Kate surprised me and now you have done. Perhaps it's in the family.'

'Possibly, possibly not. It's because I wanted to explain the family—so often a tedious recital—that I felt you needed some refreshment. Thank you, Miss Bancroft. Is there any water in that gin? Not yet? What do you say, Mr Dekker?'

'No water this morning, thank you. Well—*Salut!*'

'No. *Cheers!* came from Mrs Dragby, who sipped her sherry, before going on. 'At least Katherine is keeping you running after her. She's not running after you as so many of these silly girls do now. But I must tell you at once, Mr Dekker, I have no idea where she is.'

'As I said, she's still in England. And now I feel fairly certain she's staying in the country with a relative, probably one of her aunts.' With what he hoped was a charming smile, with the gin helping, he continued, 'I'd be very grateful if you could tell me about her other aunts.'

'That is what I promised you. We were five sisters originally, all very different. Cynthia, Katherine's mother, died in a car accident together with her husband, many years ago. So now there are four of us. The one who comes next to me is Sybil, very different from me. She is a clever and quite ruthless female predator, who marries men with money and then gets rid of them when they bore her—'

'A kind of avenger really—down with male chauvinist pigs—'

Mrs Dragby frowned. 'Not the kind of language we use in our Movement, Mr Dekker. But I'm afraid that Sybil is no use to you because she divides her time between France and America, having ample funds in both countries. Now that only leaves Leonora and Betty, and I must say I'm surprised if Katherine is staying with them, because they are two of the silliest women in England. Leonora—Mrs Fentley, divorced—has spent her time chasing impossible men. She sees herself as a *femme fatale* out of a cheap women's magazine. Betty— not married, she's Miss Rainer—devotes herself to animals, chiefly dogs—'

'I find it hard to imagine Kate going off to live with those two,' said Dekker out of his disappointment.

'So do I. But you ought to pay them a visit. They may easily know something about Katherine that I don't know, being so completely out of touch. Without a single clue to her whereabouts, Mr Dekker, you're a begger who can't afford to be a chooser. And don't give it up. That could be bad for both you and Katherine. Now make a note of the address of Leonora and Betty.

It's the Dower House, Little Paddleham, near Cranberry, Bucks. Have you got that?'

'I have, thank you.'

'But I warn you—they're a pair of geese—'

'Well, one has to take a few tame geese while on a wild goose chase.' He swallowed the rest of his gin. 'You've been very kind, Mrs Dragby. And please take care of those watercolours.' He had another look at them in the reception room, while trying the goose joke on Miss Bancroft. She smiled but then she had been smiling all the time.

'Do you know about trains, Miss Bancroft?'

'I have to, Mr Dekker, because Mrs Dragby accepts many speaking engagements.'

After a brief delay, she told him that he could catch a train to Cranberry at 1.55. And he did.

Twelve

ROUND ABOUT 1.55, Kate, Sybil and Marcel were sitting on the lawn, taking coffee after lunch. Marcel, driving a noisy little French sports car, bright red, had arrived just before lunch. He was wearing a Hollywoodish blazer with no lapels or buttons and charcoal linen trousers, which Kate coveted at once. All that he had brought from the childhood she remembered were his arched eyebrows and solemn round dark eyes. Now he had a beard, short and square, but no moustache, and being deeply tanned he looked rather like a Pharaoh about to worship the sun. He was not unattractive, and Kate was prepared to enjoy his company, even though he did talk about films all the time and was very solemn about them in a French-Hollywood style.

'You see,' he was telling them, 'I am working now with Dogle, who is both producer and director of this picture—and I am his assistant—'

'Why is he called Dogle?' asked Sybil.

'Because it is short and is not his name. He is half-

Syrian, half-Swiss.'

'That must have taken a bit of doing,' said Sybil.

Marcel ignored all such interruptions. 'This is the first time I work with him. I am to be with him on the floor and do some second-unit shooting. But now I am landed with the script, which he is tearing to pieces and trying to find new ideas for it. He bought the story him-self—it is a best-seller about a girl who falls in love with her uncle—but now it is too thin and slow for him. So there must be ideas—his ideas of course. When I left him in Hollywood he was wanting a rodeo—' He paused in sheer disgust.

'Was the girl or the uncle going to be in it?' Kate asked. 'The rodeo, I mean.'

'Nobody could be in it,' Marcel declared. 'It was a complete imbecility. Dogle must have been looking at some old Western on television late-show. But now I have had a cable, and he has had another idea. He de-mands a scene where a madman uses a whip on three naked girls until they bleed—'

'Oh—what a horrible idea, Marcel!' cried Sybil.

'It is what they like now all the time,' he told her gloomily. 'How happy I would have been if I had been born forty years sooner, working in the Thirties—*Carnet du Bal*—*La Femme du Boulanger*! But now they want nudity, whips and blood. There is no such scene in the story of course. So how do I bring in this madman and his three girls? You can think of something perhaps, Kate?'

'No, Marcel, not a hope.'

'Kate is wondering if her civil service boyfriend is just sitting about drinking too much gin,' said Sybil.

Not Dogle himself, with the Syrian half of him working at full blast, could have been more excitedly creative than Marcel now. 'But this is something. *L'administration*! *Chef de bureau*! *Fonctionnaire*! Civil servant, as you say. He is old close friend of uncle. And we need a heavy—a baddy. He is bored. He drinks all the time. He is going mad. It is late and there are three secretaries—we cast voluptuous starlets, very cheap—and he shows them a gun and makes them undress. He takes a whip to them. Why has he a whip? Never mind—later I find a whip for him. Kate, it is a *wonderful idea*.'

She pulled a face at him. 'I think it is absolutely *disgusting*.' And this gave her an excuse to leave them. She lingered by the rose bed. She stared at the row of proud irises. She was aware of the swallows swooping and darting. But she was wondering if she had made a terrible fool of herself. When she had left Tom Dekker in London, she was ready to admit that he attracted her. But now it seemed as if she had gone and fallen in love with him, chiefly because she had condemned herself to keep thinking about him, going back over every word that had passed between them. And yet of course, for all she knew, he might be sozzling away in that horrible pub, never giving a further thought to that idiotic—and quite unfair—challenge of hers. It was all very well for Sybil, the tough old campaigner, to keep saying 'Don't weaken', but she wasn't in her twenties and already half-lost in love. Kate looked at the rest of the garden with eyes that were beginning to prickle and smart.

Thirteen

DEKKER WAS ABLE to book a cheap day return to
Cranberry, Bucks. On principle he now spent as little
money as possible on railway travel. He was dead
against these nationalised concerns that did not try to
meet their rising costs by attracting more customers. All
they did was to raise their rates and charges every few
months. He had half a mind to heighten his protest by
not buying a ticket at all, dodging about the corridors
on the outward journey and then, returning to London,
lingering on the platform until the collector abandoned
his post. He was still sketching some further devices
when he took a seat in an empty second-class carriage.

The train had started to shiver and grumble when the
young man hurriedly joined him. 'Just made it,' he told
Dekker triumphantly. This remark seemed completely
out of character for the young man had long hair and a
heavy beard and might have been John the Baptist on
his way back to the locusts and wild honey. On the
other hand, he was not wearing jeans and an open shirt

[66]

but a business suit and a collar and tie. He was also carrying an attaché case that had given up trying to look like leather. Dekker regarded him with some curiosity, but said nothing until the young man, sweating a little, had mopped his face.

'Not a good afternoon for hurrying to catch a train,' said Dekker companionably.

'Right! Too bloody warm! But I like names if we're going to talk. Osbert Fewly.'

Dekker was tired of J. Carlton Mistletoe. After hesitating a moment, he leant forward and almost in a whisper announced himself as Theodore A. Buscastle. 'The A. is for Amadeus—honouring Mozart.'

Fewly showed no surprise, though indeed he had not left himself much face to show surprise. However, after a sharp look, he said 'Not connected with National Adhesives, are you?'

'Well now, that's a question, isn't it?' But asking more as Buscastle than as Dekker. After an idiotic pause, he went on, 'But as a matter of fact I'm not. And never have been. Don't really know anything about National Adhesives.'

'Been in the news a lot lately.' Fewly sounded suspicious.

'I don't read or listen to the news very often.' This was more Dekker than Theodore A. Buscastle.

'Then you ought to, Brother,' said Fewly.

'Possibly you're right, Brother.' This was Buscastle replying.

'You're democratic, aren't you?'

'Sometimes I am, sometimes I'm not.' This was Dekker's answer, just for the hell of it. Half a suburb joggled past before Fewly spoke again. He was probably wondering if this was a Brother in whom he could confide. But Dekker felt that Fewly was full of himself, proud to be taking this train, and so was really eager to talk. So Dekker waited, though putting on a Theodore A. Buscastle face.

'I'm a shop steward at the Camberwell branch of the Gum Division of National Adhesives,' Fewly began importantly, 'and I've been selected to attend, though not as full-voting member, this meeting of the National Adhesives Executive.'

'I congratulate you. Especially if you were chosen by a definite democratic process—'

'Sure I was. Completely democratic, Brother. We always have been in Gum, though I've heard some funny rumours about Glue and Paste.'

'But don't you all have to stick together?' Dekker felt ashamed of himself. He was beginning to sound like a stand-up comedian, a type he detested.

But Fewly went straight on. 'Yes, I got the votes—show of hands, of course—to attend this special meeting of the National Adhesives Executive. Now this meeting is to confirm that unless we get the forty per cent rise we've asked for, then we take industrial action—'

'In short, you stage a strike, in plain old language—'

'Call it that if you like, Brother. A simple issue—nothing could be simpler. If we can't get a living wage, then we walk out. Democratically arrived at, mark you.'

'Show of hands?'

'It was at our Branch. Practically unanimous. A straightforward demand. Forty per cent on the pay, shorter hours, and longer holidays. That's all we ask.

[68]

Nothing could be simpler.'

'And all democratically arrived at?' But this was more Dekker than Buscastle.

'I told you that.' Fewly took a sharper tone. 'Same at our Warrington Branch. And right across the board finally at the National Adhesives Executive. You got any objection, Brother?'

'Yes, I have.'

'What?'

'*I* wasn't there.'

'But you said you'd nothing to do with National Adhesives.'

'I haven't—until they want much more money for much less work. Then I come in. After all I'm a tax-payer. And I don't want to pay more taxes to keep gum, glue and paste going.'

'Here—you must be joking—'

Theodore A. Buscastle took over. 'Quite right, Brother. Fact is, I'm a great joker. You ask them at the Cranberry Constitutional Club. All the same you haven't explained why you're being sent—in a non-voting capacity—to this National Adhesives Union Executive Committee's special meeting. I want to hear about that— all in confidence, of course, Brother.'

'Give your word?'

'Certainly.'

'We're into a difficult scene now. And either me or the chap from our Warrington Branch will have to speak up for Gum. You see, Brother—' and now he lowered his voice—'differentials have been brought into it this last week. Glue started it—'

'I'm not surprised,' Dekker murmured.

'Maybe not, but it surprised us in Gum. Okay, if there's going to be differentials, Gum comes first, not Glue—'

'How about Paste?'

'Not in the running. Doesn't even pretend to be. You can forget Paste—'

'I might or I might not,' said Dekker, just to keep things going.

Fewly ignored this. He was a great ignorer. 'It's all between Gum and Glue. You might find a lot of this technical, Brother.'

And indeed Dekker found it very technical, so much so that he lost interest and began staring out at the sun-lit fields and farms and the inevitable patches of wasted ground that went flashing past, while Fewly went droning on and on. Finally, when the train began to check its speed and his watch told him he must be nearing Cranberry, he got up, tapped Fewly sharply on the shoulder and spoke to him with a new eloquence.

'Brother Fewly,' he began, 'I must tell you before we part that I disagree with you entirely. If there must be differentials, then they must go to Paste. Yes, Brother— *Paste*! It is Paste, the despised, humble yet urgently necessary Paste that should have fifty per cent added to its pay packet, should not work more than thirty hours a week, and should be given six weeks holiday, to be spent, I trust, in eating fish and chips in Torremolinos. I get out here,' he concluded severely. 'So good afternoon, Brother!'

There were several people waiting to give up their tickets at the exit, so Dekker, to save time, spoke to a young porter who was leaning against a notice board and eating an apple.

'Please can you tell me how far it is to Little Paddleham?'

'No, I can't,' said the young porter. He was an oaf to look at and he spoke like one.

'Why can't you?'

''Cos I never heard of it.'

'Yes, you have.'

'Have what?'

'Heard of it. It's called Little Paddleham. I just told you.'

The oaf porter rejected part of his apple by spitting it out. Then he said derisively, 'Very funny. I'm laughing me head off.'

'Perhaps you wouldn't miss it.' And Dekker moved to the exit. Outside he found an old taxi and a grumpy elderly man standing beside it.

'Do you know Little Paddleham?'

This did nothing to improve the driver's day. He waited a moment and then said sulkily, 'Bin there—yes.'

'Like to take me there?'

'Not go give meself a treat, I wouldn't. Cost you a pound—and no argument.'

'Very well, let's go. The Dower House. But I may want you to wait.'

'30p for every 10 minutes—'

'Isn't that expensive?'

The driver forgot to sulk. 'We have inflation here,' he said proudly. 'Dower House, you said, didn't you? Want to watch it there, mister. House full of bloody dogs.'

They went along lost lanes and past dwindling remnants of an ancient rural England. Finally, they arrived at what had once been an impressive entrance gate, now half-rusted away.

'Dower House,' the driver announced. 'An' seen better days—like a lot of us. You want me to wait? All right. But this is where I'm staying. There's one dog in there the size of a bloody pony—an' no error. So watch it, I say.'

However, no dogs of any size were to be seen in the garden, only a woman snipping away at rose bushes.

Fourteen

SHE WAS WEARING tight indigo pants and an emerald shirt, above which her fierce auburn hair looked unbelievable. When she turned he saw that she was middle-aged, though wildly pretending not to be, and had a long nose and a hungry look. Dekker felt sure at once that this must be Aunt Leonora, Mrs Fentley, the chaser of impossible men.

'I must say you don't look like a plumber,' she began, 'even though it's so hard to tell nowadays—'

'Sometimes I wish I were a plumber,' he told her, smiling. 'Then I'd be urgently needed—'

'You would be here. All the hot water we've had for the last three days has come out of a kettle. But if it's anything about dogs, it's my sister you're looking for—'

'I want to see her, but I'd like to talk to you first, Mrs Fentley. My name's Dekker—Tom Dekker—and I'm a friend of your niece, Kate—'

'Look—if this is going to take any time, let's sit in the summer house, so that I can cool off. I'm boiling. I'll

[73]

lead the way.'

It was a very small summer house. Moreover, only one side of it offered them seating. The result was that they were sitting close together while Dekker told his story, and indeed before he had finished it he found he must have moved even closer, so that another trousered thigh was pressing against his. If this had been Kate it would have been very pleasant indeed, but such close contact with her Aunt Leonora, very warm and smelling rather like a pile of old magazines, was quite a different matter.

'My God!' she cried, when he had explained his quest, 'aren't you a silly-billy?' Though she gave him a wide smile. 'And of course it sticks out a mile.'

'What does?'

'That the wretched child is far too immature for you, Tom. It *is* Tom, isn't it? Name I've always liked. The whole idea is of course quite childish. I'm surprised you didn't tell her not to be ridiculous. You're an attractive man—you know that, don't you? —and you don't have to go charging round the country to satisfy a silly girl's whim.' Now she put a hand, long and fierce, on his arm.

'Why do you call Kate *a silly girl*?'

'Now don't think for a moment I dislike Kate.' She gave his arm a squeeze, and there may have been more thigh pressure. 'I'm quite fond of her—always have been. But can't you see how immature she is? What real experience has she ever had? Writing a play, you say? How absurd—with her background! One year of a foolish little marriage—and then what? Sociology—I ask you! Now if I ever started writing plays—or novels —well, you can imagine, my dear Tom.'

[74]

And her dear Tom could too. He tried a quiet wriggle but found he was up against an arm rest on his right side, with his left side almost taken over and occupied by Leonora. To cover his confusion, he said, 'Does your sister think that Kate is immature?'

'What—Betty? She wouldn't think the average twelve-year-old immature. Her idea of immaturity is any puppy not properly house-trained. But look—why don't I take you into the house to talk to Betty—while I get out of these rags and try to look presentable? She's indoors this afternoon because she's waiting for a phone message from the vet. Come along, Tom.'

But even on their way to the house she took his arm and squeezed it. The house was longish and low, was filled with knick-knacks, and had an overall smell that reminded him of a zoo. Betty received him in what was apparently her own sitting room, packed with photographs of animals, mostly dogs. And indeed as he had walked with Leonora across the hall he had heard a devil of a lot of barking. Betty put him into a small armchair, with his back to the door, while she settled down on a fat little sofa with a fat little peke in her arms. She herself had round eyes, a round face and figure, all vivid but not quite real, rather like an illustration in a children's book. However, she listened, quivering with sympathy, to his account of himself, even though no animals came into it.

'Oh—poor Mr Dekker,' she cried. 'What a shame! We haven't the least idea where Kate is. We were only talking about her last night—such a sweet clever girl—and wondering what she was doing these days. We don't see much of her now. She and Leonora don't really get along, Kate being so much younger and more attractive.'

She started playing with the peke. 'No, that's *naughty*, Leo. If you do that again, Mother will be cross.' She smiled at Dekker. 'You're fond of dogs, aren't you, Mr Dekker?'

'Only occasionally,' he told her dryly. 'Most of 'em are far too fussy. Like having a drunk in the room.'

'Oh—that's because you don't *understand* them. I love them all—the darlings.'

To change the subject, he said, 'I got your names and addresses from Mrs Dragby—'

'And how did you like Mildred?'

'Didn't expect to, but in fact I did. But now I'm worried. You three Aunts don't know where Kate is, yet it's ten to one she must be staying with an aunt, and that leaves only her Aunt Sybil, and I'm told she doesn't live in this country. So where am I?'

'Kate may have gone abroad to join her. No, Leo, don't be stupid.'

'No, I forgot to tell you that Kate told me quite definitely she was staying in England—'

But a noise at the door turned Dekker round. The most ferocious-looking dog he ever remembered seeing had entered the room—some sort of mastiff—and was now staring, bristling and growling at him. He felt his stomach crawling, perhaps trying to get out of the room on its own.

'This is Tutu,' cried Betty, delighted to welcome the brute. 'And don't think he's unfriendly. He's really most affectionate—aren't you, darling?—only he's rather nervous when he first meets a stranger. So please don't make a sudden noise or an abrupt disturbing movement.'

'Not even to wipe the cold sweat off my brow?'

'You know that's silly. What were we saying? Oh—yes—about Kate and Sybil—'

'Yes, about Kate and her Aunt Sybil. Most important. But first, do you think you could suggest to Tutu that he leaves us? I haven't really time to get to know him—'

Dekker had an ally now in Leo the peke. Fixing his large flat eyes on Tutu with more courage than real lions appear to have, Leo directed at the brute three defiant yelps.

'Go on then, Tutu,' said Betty. 'Kennel.'

Turning his head slowly, Dekker watched Tutu's every inch of departure. Immediately then the room enlarged itself and suggested a pleasant and useful exchange of information and ideas. 'Everybody assumes that this Aunt Sybil is still living abroad. But suppose she isn't and has come back here, and that's why Kate is staying with her. Kate might never have moved out at all if she hadn't accepted an invitation from this Aunt Sybil. And I don't even know Sybil's name—'

'Sometimes I find it very confusing myself because of all her marriages and divorces. I seem to remember an animal comes into it. Badger, beaver, otter, fox? Oh—look who's come to see us!'

Dekker did, only to mutter, 'Oh for God's sake!' Either here was an outsize Irish wolfhound or something out of science fiction. He seemed to fill half the room. And in another frisky moment he might wreck it.

'You'll see, Mr Dekker, Tiny's so sweet and affectionate—aren't you, darling?—and this is nice Mr Dekker—'

But Tiny did not hold out a giant paw to be shaken but promptly climbed all over Dekker and began giving him a wash-and-brush-up with an enormous tongue.

Dekker was determined to learn Aunt Sybil's name, and now had to keep the talk going throughout this affectionate wrestling match with Tiny. 'Badger, beaver, otter, fox—you said, remember? Now, please, which is it?'

'It's fox—yes, it is.'

'Just fox? It's a fairly common name. Tiny, turn it up now, old boy?'

'No, it's not just fox. It's one of those uncommon American names that suggest they've been roughly translated from German. It has something tacked on that you don't do to a fox, do you see?'

'I'm afraid I don't. The point is, I don't do anything to foxes, not even hunt 'em.' He pushed most of Tiny to one side.

'I remember now.' Betty's tone was triumphant, and Dekker knew she really had it. 'Foxbeater—she was Mrs Irving Foxbeater when she married that American. I can't imagine how I came to forget it.'

'Not easy, certainly. So now I must assume that Mrs Sybil Foxbeater has come back to England and Kate is staying with her somewhere in the country—'

'Well, I don't know. Kate has some second cousins on her father's side—'

Dekker almost groaned. 'Oh—no—no, no, no! Second cousins are *out*. Kate wouldn't stay with second cousins. Nobody stays with second cousins, except the French aristocracy in Proust. Now it's Mrs Sybil Foxbeater—or nothing—'

'We can decide that together outside this dogs' home.' But this was Leonora bursting in on them. 'Don't be an idiot monster, Tiny. I'm taking this nice man away.' And she pulled Dekker out of his chair and took him along to her own sitting room, rather smaller than Betty's. It had photographs everywhere and reproductions of Toulouse Lautrec's posters along the walls. She took him straight across to a small settee and a return to thigh pressure.

She was wearing a dark magenta dress cut low between her breasts and ending at the knee, exposing rather stringy legs. Her face, not a small one and now in full war paint, with plenty of green eye shadow and geranium lipstick, was coming so close to his that he seemed to be looking at a bad gouache landscape. Now she took both his hands, toyed with their backs a few moments, then turned them over to examine his palms.

'As I thought, Tom,' she began, 'you're far too cautious. See how this line is joined to the lifeline. Never fails to suggest extreme caution. Chances come your way but you fail to take them. My God—you might be a solicitor!'

'Nonsense, Leonora,' said Dekker, who didn't like solicitors. 'May I point out that I'm a civil servant now on leave because I'm supposed to drink too much—'

'Don't think I don't know your kind of man. You drink too much to drown your emotional and erotic life, all that a mature woman can give you.' She squeezed both hands hard.

Suddenly she stopped being a comic character. There was too much hunger and despair in the eyes too close to his. He was sorry for her. He couldn't even suggest this without making things worse. He had to escape— he had stayed too long here anyhow—but had to do it in such a way that a little dignity might be restored to her.

'Leonora, this is important to me,' he began, and was

then able to release his hands. 'I believe now that Kate is staying with her Aunt Sybil, who must have suddenly come back to England and probably rented a furnished country house somewhere—'

'She's rich enough,' said Leonora. 'And that could explain Kate's choice. Probably they've been writing to each other all the time. Sybil has the money so she's the only aunt worth bothering about.'

'I don't see it like that, you know,' Dekker told her gently. 'My guess is that Sybil decided to try England and invited Kate to stay with her. And Kate accepted because she was tired of her ridiculous job and wanted to do some writing.'

'And didn't mind marching out of the affair you were having—'

'We weren't having an affair. We'd only just got to know each other. The challenge was an attempt to sober me up before she began to take me seriously. Oddly enough, because I've had to give a lot of thought to her, I feel much closer to her now, when I've lost her, than I did during the few times we met.'

'I'm sorry—but I think you're boring me.'

This was welcome because now he had succeeded in restoring to her a middle-aged auntish dignity. 'Sorry about that,' he told her. 'But anyhow I must go. I have a taxi waiting.'

'Better hurry. The London train leaves in thirty-five minutes.'

The taxi driver, true to form, said he might do it—and then again he might not.

'And don't give a damn either way, do you?' said Dekker. 'Well, I'll tell you a secret, my friend. Neither do

I. Not a sausage. Cranberry or London—all the same for the next two or three hours. 'But he was doing more than paying the driver in his own dreary coin. He was expressing what he was beginning to feel. Almost without hope. For where in the name of ten thousand estate agents was he to find Mrs Sybil Foxbeater? However, he caught the London train just as it was pulling out.

Fifteen

DEKKER DISLIKED SHARING compartments on a train with women and children and the kind of man who looked as if he might be a prominent town councillor. After breathing hard in the corridor, he chose a compartment that had one male occupant who didn't look as if he knew anything about municipal elections. He was brooding over a sample case when Dekker joined him, and Dekker decided he might be a salesman for something rather disreputable. His coat, a purple check job, was too large for him, his lilac trousers too tight. He had a ginger crew cut and a face so lop-sided that it could offer at the same time a narrow smile at one end and a broad grin at the other. Altogether a promising character, as a railway companion for a couple of hours, to a man now bewildered by and tired of his own thoughts: moreover, with nothing to read.

'Warm again,' was Dekker's gambit.

'You've said it. And if it's all the same to you, pal, I'm taking this coat off. The wife suggested it and I ought to have known I ought to be putting on something lighter. She hasn't a clue.' He certainly seemed happier without his coat. 'Travelling on business?'

'No. Social call. Two aunts.'

'Money there, no doubt.'

'Not a bean. By the way,' Dekker went on expansively, 'My name's Rufus Seddlebirk.'

'Saddlebank?'

'No—Seddlebirk—old Shropshire family.'

'I'm Buddy Jickson. Call me Buddy.'

'Certainly, Buddy.'

'If I call you *pal*, don't mind it—just a habit. Now from the look and chummy style of you, I wouldn't say you had anything to do with Customs and Excise—'

'And you'd be right, Buddy. I'm against 'em. The minions of greedy state robbery. With the duties now on wine and spirits, they're robbing us blind.'

'You're dead right one hundred per cent, pal. Now what would you say to a touch of gin?'

'I'd welcome it, Buddy. My favourite drink, as it happens.'

'Say no more.' And from his case Buddy brought out a bottle and glass. 'Now this is *Happy Jappy Gin*. I've just got control of the English end of it. Try it.' As Dekker did. 'What d'you think of it?'

'With respect, Buddy, as the politicians say, I'm afraid it's terrible.'

'Bit of an acquired taste. But give it another try.'

After another sip. 'Still terrible. Are they distilling it from old clothes?'

'I wouldn't know. To tell you the truth I never drink gin. I'm a whisky man myself.'

'You don't surprise me, Buddy. Now I take a lot of gin—and usually drink it neat—'

Buddy at once offered him the fascinating narrow-smile-to-broad-grin effect. 'Ah, but that's the point, pal. How many other people take it your way? Not one in a thousand. Now I'll show you something. Let's have your glass.'

He poured more *Happy Jappy* into Dekker's glass, a fat rummer type, and then took out another and smaller bottle from his case. 'Now you try it with *Geisha Gamboge Bitters*. Allow me, pal.' He shook some of the bitters into Dekker's glass, like a man doing a conjuring trick. The liquid was now, if anything, even brighter than gamboge. 'Take a good pull at it. Down the hatch!'

It made Dekker feel he was taking part internally in a Tokyo torchlight procession. However, the flavour wasn't quite so horrible. He downed the rest of it, and though the stuff was too fierce, it began to acquire a weird charm of its own. 'Much better,' he announced.

'Mark my words,' said Buddy, pleased. 'In a year's time, instead of Pink Gins everybody'll be asking for *Gamboge Gins—Happy Jappy* with *Geisha Bitters*. Now give it another try, pal.'

Buddy poured out another huge helping. Dekker told himself he ought to take it easy, so merely had a sip. 'Better—though tastes rather like an old attic—'

'Pal, this isn't Napoleon brandy. You need more of a swallow than a sip. I see it being dished out half-an-hour from closing time. Now send it down, buster.'

Dekker did, even though he began to wonder if he was going out of his mind. 'Yes, a shade better, Buddy,' he announced very carefully. 'But tell me—what's the idea?'

[84]

'Believe it or not,' Buddy began impressively. 'I can sell this *Happy Jappy*—wholesale—at eighty pence a bottle, and still make a profit.'

'Not possible, Buddy,' Dekker told him with enormous solemnity.

'Smuggling it in of course,' Buddy continued, 'bootlegging it straight off the ship.'

'What ship?'

'Japanese of course. She'll anchor about four miles, somewhere off the South-West coast. Night of course—'

'Dead of night,' said Dekker gravely. And then thought he sounded idiotic. Surely he wasn't stoned?

'Now for some straight talk. D'you know what I'm going to do, Seddlebirk?'

'No I don't.' Dekker found himself struggling with some confusion. There couldn't be anybody called Seddlebirk.

'I'm taking you into my confidence, Seddlebirk. So no loose talk anywhere—'

'Certainly not. No loose talk.'

'The Jap ship'll anchor about four miles out—exact location to be arranged—then I'll have a big fast motorboat there. You'll take on a first load—also to be arranged—of between fifty and a hundred cases—Bob's your uncle!'

'Buddy—pal—I know Bob isn't my uncle—that's just a saying—out-of date actually. But I also know—*I also know*—note this, Buddy—I shan't be in the big fast motorboat—'

'Why not, Seddlebirk?'

'Keep that Seddlebirk down—somebody may be listening—old Shropshire family, after all. What were we

[85]

talking about?'

'You said you wouldn't be in the big fast motor-boat—'

'Quite right. *You* must handle the big fast motorboat. I'll be handling public relations—'

'Not a chance, pal. I'm public relations—know 'em backward. But can't go on the water. Dead sick all the time.'

'Not me. Good sailor, like all the Seddlebirks. But can't handle the machinery. I'd be no dam' good even in a small slow motorboat, and a big fast one would frighten the life out of me. But I have an idea, Buddy pal—you might call it a whale of an idea.' And Dekker laughed heartily, surprising himself.

'I'll buy it.'

'Won't cost you a thing. Save money actually. My idea is this,' Dekker went on, trying to be solemn, no more lunatic laughter, 'we don't have a motorboat. No boat, no bootlegging. Old hat now—bootlegging. We bring the stuff in as Jappy After-Shave or Geisha Before-Shave or Samurai Hair Lotion.'

'They'd rumble us, Seddlebirk—'

'Rumble us what?'

'Seddlebirk—your name.'

Dekker put his head into a slow negative wag. 'It doesn't sound like my name. But we'll let that pass. We have an important business discussion here. It's no time to be quibbling about names.' He stood up and started swaying. 'You haven't bought the big fast motorboat yet, have you?'

'Have an option on one.'

'Get rid of it,' said Dekker sternly, 'while I go along

[86]

to the lavatory.'

He floated easily towards several lavatories, but they were all occupied. On his way back from the one he finally used, he wandered rather than floated into difficulties and bewilderment. He lost the compartment in which he had left Buddy and his *Happy-Jappy* samples. The first he tried was occupied by two women and four children and big paper bags. He had aimed at the right compartment, but in the wrong coach. But no Buddy even then, only a large man snoring his head off. After drifting disconsolately along one section of corridor after another, he more or less collapsed into an empty compartment and immediately fell asleep. Waking as the train crept into its London terminus, Dekker concluded that he had just had a dream about drinking a lot of *Happy-Jappy Gin* and *Geisha Gamboge Bitters*. But if a dream, then why did his head think it was wearing an iron helmet, and why was his palate haunted by some flavour that suggested mice playing among old clothes in an attic?

And anyhow, when and where—for God's sake—was he going to start finding Kate and her Aunt Sybil Fox-beater? He carried this query, as if it weighed several hundredweight, into the Refreshment Room, where he ordered a gin that had been distilled in London for the last 150 years.

Sixteen

'I KNEW THIS Lady Brindleways in Cannes a few years ago,' said Sybil. She was talking to Kate and Marcel after dinner on Tuesday. 'Then I ran into her at the Flower Show. She was big then and now she's enormous —ought to lose about forty pounds. She's a silly woman but quite harmless, and I gather she has a beautiful place about fifteen miles from here. Well, she sent us an invitation—I told her about you two—to a Garden Party she's giving tomorrow afternoon. So what about it, children?'

'Why not?' said Marcel. 'It might give me an idea. I am having more trouble with Dogle.'

'Is this Garden Party in aid of something,' Kate asked.

'It seems to be—yes. Some sort of political party— the National Union of Loyalists. I think she calls them NUL.'

'Null—and void,' said Kate with spirit. 'They're super-patriotic flag-waving idiots, who still talk about the Empire when we haven't got one. This Lady Thing *must* be a silly woman if she's mixed up with that lot.'

'So you don't want to go, my dear.'

'No, I'm rather like Marcel. It may give me an idea.'

'Good! So we all go—'

'I've nothing fit to wear at a posh Garden Party,' said Kate.

'Perhaps I can find something that might do, darling.'

'But I'm taller than you are, Sybil.'

'Then you show more of your legs. And they're very nice legs, don't you think, Marcel?'

'They are superb. And I am an expert.'

'There's just one thing about her name,' said Sybil. 'When she was at Cannes she was still just Brindleways. Now that's she's grander, I noticed that she's tarted into something like Brin-*lew*-ays. Got that—pom-*pom*-pom—Brin-*lew*-ays?'

'She's had to work at that one,' said Kate, pulling a face. 'And I'll bet at that she sometimes forgets.'

'I shall not attempt it,' Marcel declared. 'I shall use some flattering French.'

'Which nobody except me will understand,' said Sybil, 'and of course I shan't believe you, my dear. But I have a feeling—and sometimes I have these feelings—that we shall find it all very enjoyable.' But, as Kate reminded her afterwards, some of those feelings were not to be trusted.

The following afternoon was cloudless and very warm. They were all rather hot even before they left the house, just trying to make the most of themselves. It was easiest for Sybil of course; she wore a pearly grey dress and looked rather like a very valuable, expensive silver object. She said that Marcel suggested an early photo-

graph of his namesake, Proust, when he first moved into
high society. He was wearing a black straw hat, a
vermilion blazer, and charcoal trousers. Kate already felt
self-conscious; she was so leggy in a brown striped dress
of Sybil's, offering yards of leg when most of the women
would probably be in long dresses. And there might be
dozens of those NUL idiots giving her hard lecherous
looks. And where—oh where—was Tom Dekker now?
Probably just coming out of his horrible Carvers' pub—
already half-sloshed.

All the length of the Brindleways drive there were
Union Jacks and chaps with short-back-and-sides and
those bogus stern curving-down moustaches. The house
was enormous in an Early-Victorian castle-style, which
belonged, Marcel said, to M.G.M. in its prime. On a
terrace in front of the house and overlooking the huge
lawn, they were received by Lady Brindleways, who was
very large and impressive in salmon-pink, had no nose to
speak of but pale bulging eyes and a throaty voice, so
that the general effect was that of minor royalty in its
more Germanic days. Sybil was almost immediately
caught up in a swirl of Cannes-and-County types, so
Marcel and Kate, still leg-conscious, wriggled out of it
and stood near the balustrade, looking at the wide scene
below. There the lower classes—though now they didn't
look it—were moving between stalls, kiosks, coloured
tents, or watching a group of folk dancers, boring to
Kate and unbelievable to Marcel. On the far left, beyond
a long and gorgeous rosebed, was a second lawn, and
there the NUL chaps, together with a few daft women,
were beginning to assemble. A platform, sprouting
Union Jacks, had been erected in the middle of this

second lawn. A loud speaker was being tested. Announcements, even on the main lawn, were being bawled through those megaphone things.

'I think there is to be a meeting,' said Marcel.

'I don't think, I'm sure,' Kate told him. 'I'm also sure I'm going to keep well away from it. I've heard those idiots before. Dodging the folk dancers, who always turn out to be spectacled bank clerks in short shorts waving handkerchiefs, I'll explore the stalls and tents.'

'I have seen all that before at fêtes,' said Marcel, 'and it will have nothing for me. But the meeting is something else. It may have an idea for me. You don't mind if I go there?'

'No, of course not, Marcel. But be careful. Don't get too involved. I don't know how it is in France or Los Angeles, but here, where bloody-mindedness is all too common, meetings of National Loyalists and the like soon run into rough trouble.'

'That is too absurd, my dear Kate. What—on the precious lawns of Lady Brindle-dindle! At her Garden Party! With British class system working so hard! My dear Kate, I did not realize you are so timid. Sexually—perhaps—'

'Sexually my foot!' she told him sharply. 'I'm fastidious and loyal—not timid. But just remember that while you've been waiting upon your old Dogle with his ideas about naked girls and whips, I've been doing research all over London and have seen what can go on. So—Hitchcock-Antonioni—don't say afterwards I didn't warn you. Just don't get involved, that's all.' What she described afterwards to Sybil as 'famous last words.'

She went down to the big lawn and joined the crowd

busy buying raffle tickets for pigs, champagne and whisky, guessing weights, eating ice cream, and amusing themselves in other ways that Kate never stopped to examine. But it is useless, as she realized all over again, joining a crowd if you are not going to be one of it, losing most of your ego. A certain self-pitying melancholy creeps into your contempt for these idle-minded people. It was this feeling that moved her away from the busiest stalls and finally landed her in front of a tent by itself and attracting little attention. A notice announced that the Gipsy Queen would describe your character and read your future: Short Session 25p; Full Session 50p. Deciding that 25p was as much as she could afford, for though she was living well she wasn't earning anything, Kate went into the dim and rather smelly interior. It offered her two kitchen chairs and of course the Gipsy Queen herself, who was standing behind one chair and doing a phony bit of business with a short clay pipe.

'Sit ye down, me pretty dear, an' let me tell yer lovely fortune,' cried The Queen, who was wearing a man's cloth cap, a wig of dirty grey hair, and deep tan make-up. 'An' also let me tell yer I haven't seen a prettier piece this whole blessed afternoon.'

'Do you mind,' said Kate coolly, 'if I ask you to drop the act, which really isn't very good?'

'I know it isn't.' This in a very different accent. 'I was against it but some ass on the Entertainments Committee insisted upon it. Short or long session? 50p surely?'

'Sorry—but just 25p, please. I'm hard up.'

'Really? You weren't hard up when you bought that dress.'

'I didn't buy it. I borrowed it from my aunt, who bought it in Paris a few months ago. But what about my character and fortune? Or is it all just rubbish?'

'Usually it is, if they really think I'm a Gipsy Queen. I'll take this dam' cap and wig off. They're awfully hot-making.' She revealed a greyish trim hair-do, and of course looked quite different. 'But I'll be serious with you, my dear. I don't tell fortunes for a living—I run a rather desperate little antique shop—but I am in fact a genuine sensitive. So let's sit down. And please relax—it's important.'

'Would you like my name? It's Kate Rapley.'

'Thank you. When I'm not queening it with the gipsies, I'm Mrs Erica Faldstein. Now relax—try not to think about anything—and give me your hands.'

After several long moments, during which Kate found it hard not to think about anything, Mrs Faldstein said slowly, 'I don't pretend to understand this. But I assure you it's not the usual rubbish. What has definitely come through to me is a single word—*Lost*.'

'*Lost*?' Kate was so startled that without meaning to, she pulled her hands away.

'*Lost*.' Mrs Faldstein stared hard at her. 'I think it means something to you.'

'Well—yes—' Kate stammered—'it might—yes. But am I feeling lost—or is somebody else feeling that I'm lost?'

'A man of course.' Mrs Faldstein smiled. 'But that is nothing psychic, just a guess out of experience. Give me your hands again, please, because I might discover a little more.'

Now a quivering anxious jelly, Kate squinted at the

end of Mrs Faldstein's prominent nose.

'You are not hard-hearted, not at all, but you are rather proud, wilful, obstinate. I think you feel desperate because you have this wish for a man to find you—'

Kate couldn't keep silent a moment longer. 'Yes, I have,' she confessed hastily. 'I wasn't in love with him before—just attracted and wondering about him—but now I feel I am just because I've thought so much about him. And all the time, for all I know, he may not be bothering at all—may just have given me up—'

'I think not. Though I don't see him, I feel the *Lost* is also coming from him, because he does not know now how to find you—'

'Oh—it serves me right. I ought to send a message, but the Aunt I'm staying with, who knows a lot about men, tells me I mustn't, that if he can't find me himself, then he's not clever enough for me and that I need a clever man. Oh—I don't know what to do. Can't you tell me, please, Mrs Faldstein? Oh—yes—and of course it must be 50p now.'

Mrs Faldstein nodded but kept silent, apparently concentrating in some weird sensitive's fashion, though not —thank God!—going into a trance. Finally, she declared with some decision, 'I feel you must do nothing. Just be patient and wait. If he finds you himself, you will be happy and he will be happy. If you try to help him, all may be spoilt. So you wait. After all, that is what we women are always having to do, and—remember—we are much better at waiting than men are, always so impatient. And that is all, my dear. What you have had is two-thirds psychic and one third experience and commonsense. And very good value for 50p. You must go now because I hear people waiting outside—and I need the money.'

Without knowing where she was going, she went along the edge of the big lawn, with her back to the crowd and their raffles and stalls, until she reached this end of the terrace, well removed from that end of it which overlooked the meeting. A few yards beyond the bottom of its steps was a small gate set between thick rhododendrons. This may have been closed to Garden Party visitors, but it was where she was going, taking with her the turmoil of thoughts and feelings she had brought out of that tent. Nobody else was about, not even a gardener. Walled around by rhododendrons that ranged from a dark crimson to white—and even one bush of unimagined pale yellow—she followed a narrow path that finally brought her into a tiny grassed square, bright with borders of lupins, delphiniums, iris and foxglove. A garden seat was there and she drifted towards it.

She had already been worrying about Mrs Faldstein. Was the woman a fraud, just telling her what she wanted to know? But then if she was a fraud, how did she hit on what Kate wanted to know? And if she wasn't a fraud, then all Kate had to do was to wait—and stop worrying. And Kate told herself rather sharply that as girls and women went, K. Rapley was no worrier and enjoyed a certain reputation as a cool type. Surely Tom Dekker himself had regarded her as a cool type? So worrying was out from now on—she would be cooler than ever—and this having been decided, to her surprise and indignation, she burst into tears. Now mistily observed, all the flowers, tall and upright the lot of them, seemed to regard her with contempt. The best thing she could do now, after snapping out of it, was to go on to the terrace again and find Sybil, a stopper of lovelorn tearfulness if there ever was one.

It was several minutes, after she reached the terrace, before she found Sybil. Tea was being served at that end of the terrace, but many large ladies and important gentlemen were standing up, to look down upon but also to applaud the NUL meeting. However, Sybil was seated at a small table with a brick-red moustache-chewing Colonel Farley-Walters. 'He's the Chief Constable, darling,' said Sybil, 'and he's expecting trouble,' she added cheerfully.

'Anyhow, ready for it,' he told Kate as he passed her the walnut cake. 'Never tell with these student fellas. Might take a chance, might not. Can't do a thing unless they come barging in and play it rough. But then my chaps will be ready for 'em. Had a tip from the university this morning, so we're all set.' Obviously he liked the look of Kate and was showing-off a bit.

'By the way, my dear,' said Sybil, 'where's Marcel? Haven't you been together?'

'No, he went to the meeting while I went to have my fortune told—'

'Tall dark man and strange bed—that sort of thing, eh?' said the Colonel, ten to one a dirty old man.

'Kate darling,' said Sybil, 'wriggle through and see if you can spot Marcel. It ought to be easy—with that black straw hat and that horrible blazer.'

But it wasn't easy at that distance, the smaller lawn being packed now. And then while she was still staring hard—it happened. Shouting turned her round, and then she saw that two or three hundred young men—students, obviously—were charging across the big lawn, pulling down flags, overturning the stalls, and scattering what was left of the crowd down there. But of course they were here to interrupt and then break up the meeting. They swarmed across the long rosebed, and began fighting their way towards the platform. Soon all was confusion, a boiling pot of struggling humanity. Not only were there the student invaders (some girls among them too) and the more stalwart NUL types trying to repel them, but there were also the people who had attended the meeting out of mere curiosity and were now trying to escape from a battlefield. Some of the superior persons had now left the terrace to seek shelter in the house, so it was easy for Sybil to join Kate at her vantage point.

'What about Marcel?' Sybil shouted.

' I seemed to catch a flash of his red blazer, a minute ago, but I couldn't be sure—they're all so mixed up down there—idiots!'

'But why have all these long-haired boys come here to start fighting?'

A great shout went up. A few of the students had reached the platform and were tearing down its Union Jacks and Loyalists' insignia.

'They're from the university and are idiot extremists at the other end of the political scale—Marxists, Maoists, Trotsky-ites, International Socialists, and so on,' said Kate, close to Sybil's ear. 'I've watched them in action before—in London. Soon Colonel Thing's chaps will arrive—the police—'

'And they'll stop this nonsense,' said Sybil. 'And

about time too!'

But Kate was an expert. 'In time—yes. But it'll be a lot worse before it's better. This happens nearly every time. Both sides start fighting the police. You'll see. And look—here they come.'

A blue tide was flowing fast across the big lawn. And several police vans had managed to get in somehow, wrecking a few more stalls and tents. There were shouts, warning or defiant, from all sides. The long rosebed was now part of the battlefield and would not be its charming self again until next season. About fifty of the police— and there must have been about a hundred of them altogether—now linked arms, to advance in the direction of the platform, where the storm troops of Loyalists and Revolutionaries appeared to be behaving like maddened billy-goats and bulls. The remaining fifty police were not able to link arms, having to plunge about individually in a swirling mass of excited citizenry.

'It's really too confusing and silly,' Sybil declared, 'and I can't watch it any longer. I'm sure Marcel had the sense to get out of this and hide somewhere. He might even be already in the house, where, if Violet Brindleways has any sense, she'll be offering her special guests a few strong drinks now. And that's where I'm going. What are you going to do, dear?'

'I'll hang on here a bit. Though it sickens me—so violent and stupid.'

'You understand these things—and I don't, darling. What is the political significance of a scene like this?' Sybil asked.

'It hasn't any real political significance. Just two extreme minorities, though I wouldn't say the far Left had no influence. Even so, these students are idiots. But you go in, Sybil, and if there are any cool drinks, not too strong, save one for me.'

The police were now massing together and hauling off the worst of the combatants, and Kate felt she might have a chance now of spotting Marcel if he were still there. But now some super-idiot let off a smoke bomb and most of the scene vanished. Moreover, some of the acrid smoke was drifting her way. Enough was enough. Hurrying past Colonel Farley-Walters, who seemed to be busy with a walkie-talkie, she went by way of an open french window into the immense drawing room of the house, where Lady Brindleways, who had at least the presence for it, was holding court, and a butler and two maids were dispensing drinks. Sybil was chattering away among a group of Cannes-and-County types, and after Kate had accepted a gin-and-tonic she wandered away and looked at some rather laborious Victorian watercolours. Tom, she was sure, would have despised them, and then of course she began thinking about him.

'I say—haven't we met before?' It was a youth who combined a button-nose with a long drooping chin.

'I don't think so.' She was neither encouraging nor discouraging.

'Well, never mind—the roof's the introduction—and all that. I'm Alex Wendley—Lady Brindleways is my aunt—'

'I came with an aunt. She's over there—Mrs Fox-beater.'

'Aunts all over the place. Can I get you another drink?'

'No, thank you. But perhaps you could tell me something. Were you at the meeting?'

'Was until the rumpus started. Why?'

'I'm wondering if you noticed a French cousin of mine. He's wearing a black straw hat and a vermilion blazer—'

'Caught sight of him near the platform. Hard to miss that rig-out. But then when everybody started milling around, I cut off round the back way, into the house. Not worried about him, are you?'

'Oh—no—he must be around somewhere. But I see my aunt's looking for me.'

'Ought to be going, my dear,' said Sybil. 'Will you collect Marcel?'

'I'll have to find him first. I'll look outside. You can hang on here, Sybil.' Kate went out on to the terrace, now completely deserted, even by the Colonel. There were two or three men cleaning up the mess where the meeting had been held. But there were no NUL types, no students, no police, no vans, just a few people on the big lawn taking down what was left of their stalls. And there was certainly no Marcel within sight. She went back to report this to Sybil.

'Perhaps he was disgusted and went home,' said Sybil.

'What—and taken your car!'

'Perhaps he's just sitting in it, waiting for us. That's the most sensible explanation. Though I don't know,' Sybil went on, rather slowly, 'that this is a sensible kind of day. Days differ wildly, you know, darling.'

'Yes, I do know. And I agree with you about today. Let's make for the car. I refuse to do any more Marcel-staring.' And Kate, moving briskly, led the way down to the parking area. The car was there—but no Marcel.

Sybil was ready with a new idea. 'It's perfectly obvious what happened. He wanted to leave without bothering us, so he hired a car. Don't look like that, darling. Film people are always hiring cars. And what's fifteen miles?'

Kate had to agree. So that was that. Only it wasn't, because there was no Marcel waiting for them at home.

After they had searched the whole place, Sybil said, 'The great thing now, my dear, is not to start fussing and worrying. After Paris and Hollywood, Marcel knows how to look after himself. Possibly he's chasing some girl, though he might have telephoned or something. But then they never think—unlike us. I suggest we get out of these clothes, have our baths early, put on something loose and easy and enjoy one of my vodka martinis. Then—some delicious cold food, the women not being here. I have at least one surprise for you in my London parcel. And no fussing and worrying, my dear— a terribly bad female habit.'

Kate was sure it was. Nevertheless, while she was on her own, bathing and changing, she couldn't help *wondering* what had happened to Marcel, without of course really fussing and worrying. And, after all, hadn't she enough on her plate, recalling Mrs Faldstein's prophecies (*not* to be mentioned to Sybil) and thinking about Tom Dekker? Still it wasn't like Marcel, who was very polite, to stay away and not send a message.

They were sitting over their cocktails when Kate said hurriedly, 'What if Marcel's had an accident?'

'You're starting, aren't you? So am I. We can't help it. But then I thought he'd have asked them to ring us.'

'Not if he happened to be unconscious—'

'Why should he be unconscious?' said Sybil irritably. 'Marcel wouldn't be unconscious—he's not the type—or is he? No, don't say it—I'm being silly. But that then's what happens of course.'

Kate finished her martini. 'Look—I'd better ring up one or two hospitals. I've had to do it before—in London. It may take time, Sybil, so perhaps you'd set out the food.'

'Of course, darling. Much more *me*. But if something dreadful has happened, please don't blurt it out all at once. *Prepare* me.'

On the advice of the first hospital she tried, she rang up two others. Again, no Marcel. Nobody even faintly like him. So they were able to enjoy their delicious food without being haunted by any image of Marcel either unconscious or suffering somewhere. Indeed, as Sybil poured out the last of the Meursault she decided that Marcel was now showing-off to some idiot girl, perhaps film-struck, and as far as they were concerned he had been more than thoughtless—downright bloody rude. 'But why are you looking like that, my dear?' she continued. 'I don't use *bloody* often, but it does come in handy sometimes.'

'I wasn't thinking about that,' said Kate slowly. 'Something quite different. I'm asking myself if I haven't been completely stupid. You see, Sybil, two of the hospitals asked me if I'd tried the police.'

'*The police*? Isn't that too absurd?'

'No, it isn't.' And Kate described what had happened at the end of the meeting. 'Marcel could have been among the young men who were arrested—'

'But can you see poor Marcel fighting a policeman?'

'No, but he needn't have been. I've watched several of these affairs, and they're mostly a huge mess of pushing and shoving. Somebody shoves Marcel into a policeman, who's hot and bothered and fed up, so he grabs Marcel, who's finally bundled into a van. It can even happen to girls. I knew two.'

'Well, it ought not to happen to Marcel. I shall complain to Colonel Farley-Walters. Rather a stupid man, though,' Sybil added.

'I'll have to do some ringing up, first,' said Kate, 'just to make sure they've got Marcel.' This demanded several calls, the last of them connecting her with an Inspector Drummit, speaking from police headquarters in the county town. Apparently there had been so many arrests that smaller police stations could not cope with them.

Forty minutes later, they were facing Inspector Drummit in a bare little room smelling of disinfectant. He was a chinny man with a hard eye, and, while not downright offensive, seemed to regard them as a pair of adventuresses, probably mixed up in some French plot that Interpol had overlooked. He had a notebook and several documents as helpful props for his suspicious act.

'You say this Marcel Danerveau is your stepson,' he said, staring hard at Sybil.

'Yes. I married his father twenty years ago.'

'But you say you're a Mrs Foxbeater—'

'There was a divorce, and then I married Mr Irving Foxbeater, an American—'

'And is he with you?'

'No, there was another divorce.'

The Inspector seemed to take a deep breath. Even Kate began to feel she too might be an adventuress, possibly in the drug racket.

Sybil decided to carry on. 'My stepson has nothing to do with these students or with any English political party. He works in films and has just returned from Hollywood—'

'Anything to prove that?'

'I haven't here at the moment, but *he* must have—cables and things. Look—I'm tired of this—'

'I'll bet you're not as tired as I am,' said Inspector Drummit, 'and the night's young yet—we can't move for all these young tearaways we've had to bring in. Higher education!' he ended in disgust.

'Look—is your Chief Constable, Colonel Farley-Walters, here?'

'For once—he is, without his dinner too and not in the best of tempers—'

'Neither am I. But I was with him this afternoon at the Garden Party, and so was my niece, Miss Rapley. He's bound to remember us. Even if he's too busy to see us, perhaps you could take a message. You really are making a mistake, you know, arresting Marcel—and I don't want to bring in the French Embassy—'

'I'll take a message, Mrs—er—Foxbeater.' And off he went.

'Sybil, I thought you were smashing,' Kate told her, piling it on a bit.

'I don't think I did badly, darling. But—my God!—thank heaven it's not the French police we're having to deal with! They're the end. Well, all we can do now is to wait. And I hope we won't be too long in this smelly little room.'

They were there for the next ten minutes. When Inspector Drummit returned, he looked and sounded just as suspicious as ever, in spite of the message he brought. 'The Chief Constable says that if you will identify your stepson and will be ready to vouch for him if it should be necessary, he can go. He hasn't been charged yet, anyhow. Half of 'em haven't. Follow me.'

He led them along a corridor and then down some steps, towards a tremendous din, behind a door guarded by two constables. The Inspector himself opened the door, bellowing for silence, which he didn't get for about a minute or so because the place was packed with young men singing *Alouette*. The chorus was under the direction of Marcel who had a black eye, a wrecked straw hat, and a vermilion blazer with one sleeve missing. As he joined Sybil and Kate he was all enthusiasm.

'I'm sorry I could not tell you what had happened, but it was not possible. But it has been wonderful,' he told them on the way out. 'I must phone a night letter to Dogle. I have several splendid new ideas. The uncle the girl is in love with goes to an English university to teach American history. The girl follows him. There is a meeting that becomes a battle like today—only bigger— we use a thousand extras. There is an attractive young American among the students who rescues her from the police. He falls for her. She falls for him. They go to bed. The uncle, who is going mad, discovers them. All this will go into the night letter cable to Dogle.' He was still at it when they got into the car. 'Tomorrow I go to this university to make notes. You see, what I need now—'

'Oh—shut up, Marcel,' Sybil told him crossly. 'We're

tired, aren't we, Kate?'

'I am and I'm sure you must be, darling. We're glad you're out of there, Marcel, but just inflict your film plans tonight on your Dogle. We've had enough of everything today.'

She and Sybil went to bed almost at once, leaving him, still wearing his ruined blazer, to face the frustrations of sending that night letter to Dogle.

Seventeen

DEKKER HAD SEATED Madge at the very same table, at ugly old Carvers', where he and Kate had sat, the night she issued her challenge. He went to claim ham sandwiches for them both, a lager for Madge and a large gin for himself, leaving her to glance through the fashionable magazine she had brought with her. 'I refuse to *look* at this horrible place,' she had told him. 'That new advertisement for cider makes everything else look even worse. I swore I'd never come here again—and look at me!'

'I apologise, my dear Madge,' he had replied. 'But it has to be Carvers' today. It suits my sombre mood. No, I'll explain later.'

Now that he was back with the sandwiches and drink, she pointed an accusing finger. 'What's that you've brought for yourself?'

'That? Just a large gin.'

'You told me on the phone, the other day, you were on the wagon.'

'I was. I am—only it's acquired a licence. No, Madge, listen. I hate to admit it, but I'm stumped. That's why I had to ring you this morning. Yesterday evening finally dished me. Do eat and drink while I tell my wretched tale. Wretched—even though it contains an extraordinary coincidence. Now Kate hadn't left a clue behind her, as you know, poor girl. The only thing I could do was to concentrate on this Aunt Sybil, who had taken a house in the country somewhere and had invited Kate to join her. But where—where? So I rang up Aunt Mildred, Mrs Dragby—a decent old warrior—and asked her if Sybil had any friends left in London—'

'Of course. I ought to have thought of that,' said Madge, munching away.

'She could only think of one. An American woman called Mrs Bentliff Brown, living at a daunting address in Mayfair. I phoned several times, finally caught her in, and she told me I could call on her at quarter-to-six yesterday afternoon. I fished out the only gentlemanly suit I've got, and off I went. I found her in a tall thin house—a tall thin woman with blue hair, a wide smile but a hardish eye. I couldn't tell her the whole daft story, but I did say I was trying to find Sybil Foxbeater's niece, staying with her somewhere in the country. Did she know where? No, hadn't a clue, didn't even know Sybil was back in England. Dead end there, as usual. Perhaps pulled a long face—I don't know—but then she laughed, offered me a drink, and said I mustn't go just because she was expecting some people at six. Now though I've taken to behaving like a fool lately—I mean about Kate, not booze—I'm not entirely a fool and it was obvious there was some point in my staying to meet these people.

I'm not boring you, am I, Madge?'

'No, I'm waiting for the coincidence.'

He swallowed half his gin. 'It's on its way. Five Americans arrived, three men, two women. After a minute, there seemed to me more of them, the two women talking so hard, the men so large and hearty, oil men, I believe. There were introductions of course, but the only name I caught—'

Madge delightedly jumped in. 'Don't tell me it was Foxbeater,' she squealed.

'Mr Irving Foxbeater himself—no less! Yes, Sybil's last husband-that-was. Oldish but a bulldozer of a man, if you can imagine a bulldozer with an enormous flat face like an unbaked pie. Mrs Bentliff Brown must have said something to him—though what I don't know, there was such a devil of a din—but he brought a hefty bourbon for himself and a gin for me—and bulldozed me into a corner. Then he knocked me out with one punch. "Last time I heard from Sybil," he said with a grin as wide as Texas, "she was still living in France. And I don't know anything diff'rent, boy." And he roared with laughter. He needed this laugh—though God knows why—after every twenty or thirty words.'

'I've just met two or three of that sort,' said Madge, 'and you can have them.'

Dekker finished his drink and got up, clearly to fetch another.

Madge put out a hand to push him down. 'No, you don't. You can't really need one, and anyhow you haven't finished your story.'

'No, but it ends miserably. He made me feel like a feeble Englishman, bleating away while he bellowed and

roared, twice as large as life and probably pulling in
another hundred thousand dollars every couple of days.
I had to explain it wasn't Sybil but Kate I was looking
for.'

'Had he met Kate?'

'Yes, a few years ago when he and Sybil were passing
through London, on their way to Noo York. "Too tall
for a doll," was his comment, "but a dish, boy—a dish
already. Worth chasin', that's for sure." But I put it to
him, in a few last bleats, that there might be some part of
England that Sybil specially cared about. But—no dice.
The Sybil he remembered didn't give a damn about the
English countryside—ha ha ha—ho ho ho! And—boy—
did she take him to the cleaners! By this time I felt I'd
been taken to some kind of cleaners myself and had
come out a miserable little object. I tell you, Madge, this
little party finally dished me. They were all quite decent
in their way of course but all so loud and self-confident
and the men so massive that I felt like an inquisitive,
futile, defeated midget. I've grown a few inches since,
but the defeat's still there. I haven't another move I can
make.'

'What about estate agents?'

'Hopeless. There are hundreds of 'em—drive you
barmy—and even then Aunt Sybil might not have rented
the house through an agent.' While he talked he idly
turned the pages of the magazine she had pushed aside.

'Couldn't you try an advertisement?' Madge was
doing her best.

'If I addressed it to Aunt Sybil—and she saw it—she'd
show it to Kate and then I'd seem a poor sort of chump
—'

'Well, I'm disgusted with Kate. I call it damned unfair treating you like this—'

'Hold it, Madge!' He was staring at the magazine. 'A last wild chance is worth a few pounds. Now look—I'll give you a fiver for this page of the magazine—'

'What are you talking about? You can have the page for nothing, if you must have it.'

'No, no, that won't do.' He ripped out the page and then produced a five-pound note, which he pushed into her hand. 'No, do please take it, Madge. It's a wild idea, and I refuse to explain it because I might discourage myself. Tell you afterwards, of course. Another drink?'

'No, I must get back to work, wondering how I'll spend these five pounds. And thank you for them—and the sandwiches. And—Tom—cheer up!'

'I am cheered up, my dear Madge. It's probably daft but it's an idea, a sudden palm tree in the desert.' He walked her to the door, went on to the bar and collected a large gin, then returned to the table and examined the page from the magazine. The advertisement read: *You can still eat in France at home if you shop at Elysée, Curzon Street, W.1. Friandises françaises. French delicacies. Prompt attention to orders by post.* He would take a look at the place this afternoon, just a scouting job, but the real attempt, the plan, the operation, must be postponed until tomorrow morning, when he would be wearing his one gentlemanly suit.

Eighteen

IT WAS TWO days after the Garden Party. Sybil had gone to bed rather earlier than usual, saying she wanted to begin reading a new American novel, though Kate suspected this was not the whole truth. Sybil, she felt, wanted to leave her alone with Marcel, who was now changing the lighting of the small sitting room, which they all preferred after dinner to the much larger drawing room, to set up a seduction scene. He had even found some suitable music on the radio and had been clever enough to turn it down so that it was just seductively audible. His black eye was now purple and rather suited him. He was wearing a pale grey arrangement, which looked as if it were trying to turn into a uniform, perhaps belonging to the life guards of some Californian super-star; and even this was fetching rather than absurd.

'You would like more Calvados?' he asked her, almost in a murmur.

'No, thanks. I don't think I can finish this helping. It's really too strong for me.' She replied in a bright tone. to break out of the scene.

'Then please allow me to finish it for you,' Marcel

went murmuring away, well into the scene. 'I love Calvados, and if your lips have touched it, then I love it even
more.'

If this was the kind of dialogue that pleased his Dogle,
then Kate felt even further removed from that master of
moving pictures. She was tempted for a second to make
a rude noise, just to bust up the seduction scene before it
turned into a wrestling match. But she liked Marcel, in
spite of his endless film talk, and she didn't want to
humiliate him. After all, he was a long way from his
usual surroundings. And then, hadn't Sybil, who had
been sweet to her, deliberately left them alone, perhaps
after an appeal from Marcel? So she kept silent, after that
Calvados dialogue, pretending to stare at a horrible
picture that the brigadier-owner must have brought back
from India. Even when Marcel, after more Calvados,
moved his smaller chair alongside hers—though recog-
nizing a familiar gambit—she went on staring in silence.

He took her hand, fondled it for a few moments, then
took both her hand and his down to her knee, another
move well-known in London as well as in Paris and Los
Angeles. Well, well, what now? She didn't want him to
start making love to her, felt no desire for him at all; but
she felt just sufficient response to the seduction scene,
sapping her will to resist, not to be able to tell him she
didn't want him and that he mustn't expect any familiar
answering moves from her. She wondered afterwards,
being honest with herself, what would have happened
if he had allowed them to drift on without a word being
said, just with a hand creeping up her thigh or touching
her breast. But he had to talk—a very different and fatal
move.

[113]

It was only in a low voice at first. 'What we need now
—you and I, *mon ange*—is *Sex*.'

Kate sat up. 'Speak for yourself.'

He still kept to a low persuasive tone, dripping sympathy. 'No, it is for you also. You are worried. So am I.
You have problems with your play. I also with my film.
And we are lonely. So we need Sex together. To find
happiness in bed.'

'Stop it, Marcel.'

Now he took a loftier tone. 'You may feel you are not
very good in bed.'

'You're going from bed to worse,' she warned him,
while wondering if that was too corny for her comedy.

Ignoring that—perhaps it was a standard pun in
Hollywood—Marcel went blindly on. 'But that does not
matter. I am very good in bed. I have had great experience—Paris, Los Angeles, Rome too, though I was
younger then—and I have a complete understanding of
Sex—'

'No, you haven't—and take your hand away—that
scene's over now. We'll *talk*—and one of us is going to
talk sense. The Sex you've a complete understanding of
simply belongs to a long list of things it's nice to have—
toast and coffee in the morning, chocolate mints, a warm
bath, a good afternoon's tennis. You're probably good at
it just as you may be good at tennis—'

'It is better than my tennis. You will see.'

'No, I shan't see. Oh—yes—I long for my kind of sex.
I'm a big healthy girl who's more than half in love with a
man. But my kind of sex isn't playing tennis in bed. I
know your kind—I've been around, Marcel—and I'd
just as soon listen to the radio in a warm bath—in fact,

much sooner. Unless there's imagination and heart in it, it's nothing but acrobatics, gristle, spasms and a let-down. Imagination and heart, Marcel, and nothing less. No—listen—I haven't finished. I'm a sociologist of a sort, don't forget, and I've had to talk to scores and scores of girls. And you experts-in-bed boys, with your impersonal mechanical Sex, have played the devil with so many of the girls now. They want more and more, and become aggressive about it, really because instinctively they're looking for something that isn't there—imagination and heart,' she ended triumphantly.

'There are two reasons for this lecture,' Marcel told her. 'First, you do not find me sufficiently attractive. Maybe I am not your type. Second, you are now in-fatuated with your poor civil servant. You have given him something impossible to do—and Sybil and I have spoken of this—and so you think about him all the time. He won't find you. How can he?'

'I don't know. But he's clever—and if he tries hard—'

'I have worked with many clever drunks in films, where you cannot avoid them. Some of them are very clever, but they do not try hard. Sybil thinks your man is not trying at all. That is why she tells you not to send a message to help him. Sybil and I understand about drunks—'

'Tom Dekker isn't a drunk,' Kate shouted at him, furious now. 'And you can shut up. You don't under-stand anybody or anything—not Tom, not me, not sex, not life—nothing. No wonder films are now so bloody awful. I'm going to bed. Behind a locked door too. Goodnight!'

Nineteen

YESTERDAY AFTERNOON, DEKKER had done his
scouting job on the Elysée shop but had not ventured
inside, just trying a little peeping and peering. He knew
it was a long narrow establishment, all on one floor,
chiefly consisting of three rather narrow aisles, walled in
with French goodies. If there was a special postal
department, he would have to find it. He hadn't gone in
yesterday because he wasn't dressed for the act. Now
this morning, he was, not only wearing his gentlemanly
suit but also his best shirt and tie. He didn't look bad at
all. He spent the last few minutes in his flat attempting a
haughty manner and one of those choked-up accents
that important and superior men so often had. He fancied himself as a closer observer, when in the mood, but
he was no real actor. This chap he was trying out looked
and sounded idiotic. He would have to depend on suit,
shirt, tie, artful dialogue and any charm he could muster.
However, he did take a taxi to the shop, feeling vaguely
that it might help.

It was about half-past ten when he walked in. Not many customers yet. Was that good or bad? He didn't know. He chose the left-hand aisle, which started with cheeses and went on to soups. Hell in here for a greedy man who couldn't afford the murderous prices (not mentioned anywhere) they must charge. He loitered for a moment or two among the soups but then moved on when he was approached by a man who looked more like a consultant surgeon than a shopwalker. The aisle ended in a little open space, where you could go to two enclosed counters. One of them was for paying bills—and no use to him. But the other, which set his heart beating faster, was clearly labelled *Postal Services*. It might just as well have announced itself as *Dekker's Last Chance*.

One thing was in his favour. Nobody was enquiring about postal services. But behind the counter was a tall lustrous brunette, still haughty even in her boredom—though she may have been working out what she would wear on her honeymoon in Bermuda. What was certain —and he might have guessed that this would happen— was no little woman from Bromley, eager to serve and do her very best for a superior man with this suit, shirt, tie. Half his original plan vanished at the sight of this haughty brunette, because any attempt to seem haughtier would make him seem like a crazy character comedian. It would have to be charm, even though this wench looked as if she had been charmed and charmed in all the more expensive night clubs in the West End. Perhaps a touch of pathos sooner or later? Though that would take some working when his initial approach had to be by way of a complaint. But he was not fool enough to be lurking near the counter while wondering what his approach should be; he was pretending to consider some cooked meats at this end of the centre aisle. He would have lingered there even longer if another consultant surgeon had not been descending upon him.

'Good morning,' he said to the brunette, with what he hoped was not too ghastly a smile.

Returning from Bermuda, though anything but willing and eager, she said, 'Can I help you?' And then she closed her eyes for a moment as if to take a brief rest from this suit-shirt-tie ensemble.

Improvising wildly, Dekker took a shot at the grand manner. 'I think you might, if you wouldn't mind. Just a tiny thing. I'm here on behalf of a friend who lives in the country.' Now for it! 'Several of her orders seem to have gone astray. It's a Mrs Foxbeater—Mrs Sybil Foxbeater.'

The girl had opened her eyes, which were splendid. 'Foxbeater? Unusual name. That's why I seem to remember it. What's her address?'

This of course was IT. If he failed here, he was done for. 'Ah—but that's the point, isn't it? That's why I'm here, troubling you. I know her right address, naturally —but *do you*? If Mrs Foxbeater has been missing some of her parcels, then you may have been using a wrong address. I must check, if you'll be so kind.'

The girl seemed to take this in, but for some reason or other, beyond his comprehension, she was staring at him wide-eyed.

Dekker smiled. 'Yes, you have very fine eyes indeed, but then you must have been told that many times before. Now—please—what address have you been using for Mrs Foxbeater?'

He received a lustrous-brunette dazzling smile. 'If you'll wait a moment or two, I'll look it up—'

'And what will you look up, Miss Saxton?'

This came before she could move, and the speaker was that first consultant-surgeon-shopwalker, who probably had not liked the look of Dekker when he was dallying with the soups.

Faced with this monster and his harsh demand, the haughty spirit deserted Miss Saxton, who looked and sounded flustered. 'The address—er—of a country customer—for this gentleman.'

'Most certainly not.' It was the voice of Doom itself. 'Why should we give a customer's address to any casual enquirer? We're in a highly competitive line of business, Miss Saxton.' He turned to Dekker. 'I hope you overheard that.'

'I did,' said Dekker, 'and you've just lost an order for two packets of onion soup.' He retreated a few steps without turning away as the grim shopwalker marched off to his soup and cheese. Miss Saxton pulled a face at his back and then gave Dekker a mournful sympathetic look. Two enquirers for postal services arrived to claim her attention.

Now what? Dekker couldn't hang around there. He must keep out of the way until he had a plan. There was a third aisle he hadn't visited yet, and it had the advantage of being well away from the suspicious soups and cheeses fellow. It was—perhaps a good omen?—the department for all the sweet stuff of France, each side piled high with jams, chocolate, candied fruits, pears-de-luxe, and any number of jars and tins he didn't bother to examine. An assistant, a refined sad lady, asked if she could help him, and he told her he was trying to make up his mind. And this was true enough because as he wandered up and down the aisle, he was asking himself how far he could depend on Miss Saxton. Certainly she had pulled a face at *potages-et-fromages* and had given Dekker a sympathetic look. But he realized that his story wasn't strong enough as it stood now. A brunette with those eyes needed an appeal with more heart in it. But if he was seen speaking to her again, all might be trouble, grief and no address.

He bought a gift box with three little jars of honey in it. His first thought was to use the card that came with it but then changed his mind. The thing couldn't be easily flipped across the counter. He walked along to the entrance, where people were coming in or going out or hanging about, waiting for a friend. Keeping out of everybody's way, he opened the box, tore off some paper from the inside, and wrote in bold letters: *Need address to find my girl. Help please*! He folded it up and keeping it in his right hand, he went back towards the postal counter along the centre aisle, among the cooked meats. There was a woman nattering away at the counter. Without thinking where he was going, he moved slowly away to his left, only to encounter the suspicious shopwalker at the end of his aisle. This asked for a bold move.

Still clutching his folded note in his right hand, he raised his left hand, holding the honey box, almost under the fellow's nose, and in what was almost a snarl, said, 'You don't mind if I buy something here, do you?'

The man turned away in disgust. Dekker swung

round, saw that the troublesome woman was just leaving the counter, gave Miss Saxton a warning look and as he sauntered past her he flipped his note over the counter so that it fell on her side of it. Returning to the near end of cooked meats he was able to watch Miss Saxton pick up the note. She then moved out of sight, presumably to consult her file of addresses, but a tweedy nuisance of a man arrived and she had to attend to him. Dekker still hung around the same section of cooked meats, his heart thumping away. Tweedy nuisance left the counter; Miss Saxton disappeared again; Dekker began the slowest casual stroll seen in Curzon Street that day. Miss Saxton reappeared; Dekker started to move past the counter in slow motion; Miss Saxton flashed a glance and then looked away; but something had been shot across the counter to fall at his feet. He went back to the third aisle, among the sweets, before he unfolded the note and read it: *MRS F. THE GRANGE. ORLTON BY SEDGES NR BUNCH-COMBE GLOS.*

Praise God from Whom all blessings flow—with some to be showered on Miss Saxton!

Twenty

ACTION—ACTION—NOW! He found the sad refined
woman and begged her to deliver the gift box of honey
to Miss Saxton—'A little tribute to her fine eyes,'
Dekker added. He took a taxi to his flat, tore off the
gentlemanly suit and replaced it with old check trousers
and an old blue linen jacket, packed a small suitcase,
drank some gin and ate a thick corned-beef sandwich,
and found a bus to take him to Paddington. It was as
busy as ever. There was a cult of Paddington in some
circles, but it had never been one of Dekker's favourites.
He had to wait nearly an hour for a train that would
finally land him at Bunchcombe, Glos, and had to
exercise great restraint keeping himself out of the
Refreshment Room.

He boarded the train early but just before it moved
off he was joined by two youngish men, who were talking as they came in and then never stopped. They were
no whisperers, these two, and Dekker soon learnt that
one was called Batters and the other Riptin, that they

worked in the theatre as directors, that Batters had just come back from directing *As You Like It* somewhere in America and that he was now on his way to enjoy Riptin's production of *Antony and Cleopatra* somewhere in the West Midlands. Though pretending to be asleep, Dekker didn't miss a word they exchanged. He was no Shakespearean playgoer, but for Shakespeare himself he not only had the greatest admiration but also, something much rarer, an enormous affection, feeling that this astonishing man had been calling round for the past twenty years leaving vast hampers packed with marvels. However, he soon discovered that Batters and Riptin, though in the business of producing Shakespeare, didn't seem to share his view of this extraordinary man.

Batters had begun explaining his production of *As You Like It*, for some university town in the Middle West. 'From the first I'd cut all that boring Forest of Arden stuff. My Arden was a little town in the Middle West.'

'Modern dress then, naturally,' said Riptin.

'Not quite, old boy. About 1910. I was trying to tie it up to one of the earliest motorbike rallies in those parts. The Duke was a senior official of the rally who'd had to resign. And now listen to this. Against a lot of opposition, I insisted upon taking out all the middle seats and building an easy ramp from the back up to the apron, so the cast could enter through the audience on motorbikes—'

'Now wait a minute, Batters old son. Don't tell me you had all the cast riding motorcycles up a ramp—'

'Not possible of course. I'd only four chaps who could manage that ramp, but what with helmets and

goggles and leather togs nobody knew who they were.
They rode off on the prompt side and then after a minute
the people playing Rosalind and Celia and Touchstone
and Orlando and Jaques made their entrances.'

'What about trees and deers and all that jazz?'

'*Out*—the lot. That worked okay. After all, the people
round there had never seen any big trees or deer. Moreover, I did some original casting. Not only did I have a
young actor playing Rosalind—as they did at the
National a few years ago—but I also had a girl playing
Orlando—and I don't believe that's ever been done
before, outside girls' schools of course. Created a sensa-
tion—that and the motorbikes. I've got another year's
contract. Go back in September, taking Gilda with me
this time. You remember Gilda?'

Dekker longed to ask a few pointed questions about
this version of *As You Like It* but felt that any inter-
ruption from a stranger might shut them up. However,
very soon Riptin was explaining his new interpretation
of *Antony and Cleopatra*.

'I'm turning them on down there,' he told Batters.
'And why? Because now it's a Roman political play. The
love story was never any bloody good. Think of all the
top actresses who've played Cleopatra and always been a
disappointment. Octavius Caesar's my central character
and I've built up Enobarbus. Of course I've had to shift
things round a bit. Brought in two scenes from *Julius
Caesar*, and a friend of mine has done three extra scenes
for me—smashing! Goes like a bomb now. Better than
Brecht.'

'You don't surprise me,' said Batters. 'But what have
you done with Antony and Cleopatra themselves? Can't

cut them out altogether.'

'Of course not. That'ud be bloody stupid. I've kept 'em in—cutting a lot of course—but put years on 'em. Antony's now a senile old lecher and Cleopatra's a malicious old bag. I've produced 'em for laughs, as a relief from the serious politics. The scene where Caesar visits Cleopatra—you remember?—is a riot now. She's doped to hell and gone, and he's giving every line a satirical twist. But I mustn't spoil it for you, Batters old boy. Incidentally, we're playing to capacity, and nearly sold out for the next three weeks. Just shows you what you can do with the old Bard if you take a new contemporary approach.'

They were now coming in to Oxford, where Dekker had to change to a branch line for Bunchcombe. Taking down his case, he said, smiling at the pair of them, 'I couldn't help overhearing some of your talk. I hope *you* don't mind if I tell you I still like Shakespeare. Good afternoon.'

The train that would stop at Bunchcombe—and many another place—was a kind of ancient dwarf. It had only three coaches but quite a number of passengers, mostly of a rural parcel-carrying sort. Dekker decided on the last coach but didn't do well, landing himself in a compartment with two women and three children, probably aged between four and seven, working away at lollipops and looking sticky all over. The two women wore white summer dresses, one with pink spots, the other with blue spots. Pink was an angry type with squeezed-in features and a harsh voice. Blue was quite different, melancholy and moist, almost tearful, and spoke in a whisper. Though he didn't work hard at it, Dekker never discovered how the two women were related to one another, and, what was more surprising, what their relationship was to the three children. He never caught anything that Blue whispered, either to Pink or to the kids, but he soon had more than enough of Pink, who was for ever shouting, clutching, pulling, as if she hated children.

Dekker had started this journey from Paddington in the highest spirits—for wasn't he on his way to reply to Kate's challenge?—but he couldn't be blamed for any lowering of them on this ride to Bunchcombe. The late afternoon was still very warm; the carriage was stuffy and noisy; the train, having to stop at so many un-remarkable places, never reached any speed, so that the fields and distant hills crawled past it and were boring. Blue and Pink sat opposite each other and Dekker at the other end of the seat on Blue's side, while the kids, hot and bored, sprawled or squirmed in between the adults. Every minute or so, Pink, shouting 'Stop it—yew!' shot out a powerful hand to pull or to slap or to jerk a child's arm; and Dekker now recalled some doctor telling him that all this impatient pulling and jerking often did serious injury to young English children's arms. Perhaps it was true that the English were kind to animals but too often cruel to children.

The train had no corridor for the kids to explore. He was sorry for them, and said to the oldest, a boy, 'Shall I tell you a story?'

'No,' the boy told him.

'Why not?'

'Want to play.'

Blue gave him a faint watery smile and whispered something he couldn't catch. But Pink went straight into action, leaning forward and shaking the child. 'How can yew play, yew silly little juggins? Why don't yew let the gentleman tell yew a nice story?'

'Cos I don't want.'

She pulled him closer and gave him a sharp slap. The youngest child now started crying. The middle one squirmed around. Dekker wished he had kept silent, and stared out of the window at nothing in particular. And then, a great relief, there was Bunchcombe station. When he had taken down his suitcase, the boy put out his tongue at him, so Dekker put out a much larger tongue back at the boy.

'Well,' Pink shouted, angry as ever, 'yew don't have to be rude to the poor boy.'

Three people had alighted with him, and he let them go ahead because he wanted to talk to the man who was collecting the tickets. 'Do you know anything about Orlton-by-Sedges?' Dekker began.

'Little old Orlton,' said the man, chuckling. Very few people chuckle, except in print, but this man did. He was stout and rosy and gave the impression that he could be immensely helpful to a stranger. 'Going there, are you?'

'Yes. Need a taxi, I imagine.'

'That's right. Best have a taxi for Orlton.'

'I don't see one about.'

'Not today—no,' said the man, all smiles. 'Old Joe takes today off to visit his married daughter in Chipping Campden. Never fails. Good family man, old Joe is.' Some chuckles.

Dekker recognized the type now. He had met these chaps before. They were all smiles, helpfulness, good-fellowship, but all that comes out of them is bad news, in which they take a secret delight. 'No taxi then?'

'That's right. Not today.'

'How about a bus?'

'Every four hours. And I'll be damned if you haven't just missed one.' Chuckle, chuckle. 'A bit of bad luck that, I'd say. Every four hours—often nearer five.'

Steeling himself, Dekker said, 'How far is it?'

'Some say six, some say seven. If it's six, then they're long miles—what we call round here *stretchers*.' A lingering tender smile. 'Better start legging it and hope to thumb a lift.' Chuckle. 'Though it's not a good time of day for chances of a lift.'

Twenty-One

DEKKER'S CASE WAS light enough but now, after a couple of miles, it had turned into a hell of a nuisance. If he had known what he knew now, he would have brought an ash stick and a rucksack. The road was winding and narrow, often below high hedgerows, from which there came a sickly-musty smell together with some infernal pollen that made him sneeze. And of course he was wearing light town shoes, murderous for this job. He limped another hundred yards or so, then sat down on a pile of stones, listening for a possible lift. After about five minutes of various aches, he heard it coming his way, making an expensive snarling noise round a corner.

'Perhaps I could give you a lift.' She was a trim amused woman, not young, and she had pulled up a foreign sports car that must have cost far too much.

Standing, working on a smile, he said, 'I wish you would.'

'Where are you going?'

'A place nobody else wants to go to—Orlton-by-Sedges. And a house there called The Grange.'

This increased her amusement, he noticed sharply. 'Are you indeed? Hop in then.'

'Thank you.' Though he did no hopping, just joining her on the front seat rather laboriously, nursing his case, which looked very shabby indeed in the setting of this car. He said no more, not wishing to take the attention of the driver off this narrow twisting road.

However, she seemed to know it well. 'I believe a Mrs Foxbeater is living at The Grange. Are you acquainted with her?' He could hear the amusement trilling away.

'No,' he said rather slowly. 'I only know *of* her, having been all round the family.'

'Oh—the family. And was that exciting?'

'Not particularly—*Mrs Foxbeater.*'

'Now how did you guess that?' No looks were being exchanged, both of them watching the road.

'I wondered from the first. And that question about the family settled it,' Dekker went on. 'Who else would ask that question?'

She didn't speak for a few moments but he noticed she reduced the speed of the car, perhaps to make talk easier. 'You're cleverer than you look,' she said finally.

'I hope so.'

She laughed. 'You're Kate's Tom Dekker of course. But how did you discover where I'm living?'

'After taking a lot of trouble that landed me in dead ends, bewilderment, more and more anxiety. It's a story for a long winter evening, when the television set needs a new valve and everybody is sitting round the electric imitation log fire.'

[130]

'In other words, you're not going to tell me.'

'Not now. Perhaps never.'

'Nonsense! You'll have to tell Kate, and then she'll tell me. By the way, I don't think you know each other very well, do you?'

'No, we don't.' Dekker waited a moment. 'All hunches and instinct and intuition so far. Working on the feminine rather than the masculine principle. Though I'm a man all right.'

'I'm sure you are.'

'Talking of men, I met your ex-husband, Irving Fox-beater, the other night at a little American party—'

'Oh—how is Irving these days?'

'In the rudest health, I'd say. He wore me out in twenty minutes flat. All that shouting and laughing!'

'Don't tell me.' When next she spoke he could hear the mischief bubbling in her voice. 'Can you be jealous?'

'Possibly. Though I'm against it. Why?'

More bubbling now. 'Well, I've had a stepson of mine staying with us while you've been toiling to find us. He's French and works in films. Quite attractive in his way.'

'What d'you want me to do? Turn green? Why work at it?'

'Isn't that rather offensive?'

'Yes. But then I'm jealous.'

She laughed. 'You'll do. And I can't think why you should drink too much. You're not the kind of man who needs to drink all the time.'

'Mostly boredom and irritation. Life in the Civil Service, life in London, and the general English way of life. I've simply had to keep floating through them. But Kate, if she's really involved, might put an end to the

boredom and irritation. Together,' he added thought-
fully, 'with a reasonable allowance of gin. But I hope
she's not speaking fluent French by this time.'

'Marcel, my stepson, speaks English. And hers is now
chiefly "No. Shut up!"'

'Notwithstanding any attempts you may have made—'

'Now *you* can shut up. And I can't give Kate any good
advice. My three husbands were all rather stupid. You're
much too sharp and clever. Perhaps you will have to
write the plays. She hasn't finished hers yet. Partly
worrying about you, of course. It was I who kept telling
her not to send you a message to give you any help.
We've had so many stupid men in our family.'

'Not Mildred's Mr Dragby. He painted some dam'
good watercolours, that man, Mrs Foxbeater—'

'Sybil, please. I can't keep talking to people who call
me Mrs Foxbeater—it's too ridiculous. Well, here's the
house. It's quite a comfortable house, though full of
rubbishy stuff brought back from India. It has three
good guest rooms and you can stay in the third, Tom. I
like Tom and I'm already feeling a bit jealous of Kate.
And there she is—look—wearing her sloppiest clothes
and trying to dream up some witty dialogue.'

Kate looked up without interest at the approaching
car. But when it stopped and Dekker got out, she ran,
crying 'Oh—Tom—Tom!' and flung herself into his
arms. All this seemed quite natural. They had spent so
much time thinking about each other during their
separation.

'He won't tell me how he did it,' said Sybil, a few
minutes later. 'You get it out of him, darling, and then
tell me.'

'As I said earlier,' said Dekker. 'The full story demands a long winter evening, and by that time none of us may be on speaking terms. By the way, if you're allowing me to stay here—at least, overnight—I'd like to bag a bath quite soon. I've had a long and curiously sticky day. Triumphant of course—but too warm and too sticky. I might have been working all day packing boiled sweets.'

'Don't you want—' and Kate hesitated delicately— 'some gin?'

'Not until I'm out of my bath. I've—er—been easing off a bit lately, during my spell as a Private Eye.'

Kate squeezed his arm. Then she and Sybil talked very quickly, both at once, about domestic arrangements.

At dinner, Marcel, who had been staring at Dekker across the table for several minutes, asked him if he had ever done any acting.

'Acting?' cried Dekker. 'At the Ministry I spend two-thirds of my time acting. I have two principal roles. When the Minister and the Permanent Secretary have made a mess of something, I am brought in to take the blame—a simple idiot, not a holy fool but with just a vague suggestion of one. When I have to work with the other Departments, I do my Machiavelli—underplayed of course but with a few sinister touches. I tell you, Marcel, I do far more acting than any member of Actors' Equity.'

'I think you could play the Professor of English in my university sequence,' said Marcel slowly. 'Whimsical— but sexy. Very English now.'

'Bloody-minded many of us, rather than whimsical. I don't know about sexy. Never occurred to me.'

[133]

'It's crossed some of our minds,' said Sybil dryly.

'But no film-acting, thank you, Marcel. I'd keep changing my lines.'

'Talking about changing,' said Sybil, 'may I ask, Tom, if your intentions here are honourable?'

Solemn but twinkling, Dekker said slowly, 'To be quite honest—and I'm nothing if not honest, as you will discover, Sybil—I haven't given the matter a thought.'

'Oh—haven't you?' Kate gave him a look. 'Well, *I* have.'

Still refusing to tell them how he had found them, at least he did entertain them, over coffee, by describing with a wealth of detail the first two events in his saga: the interview with S. K. Overton-Briggs and his visit to the North Green Drama Club. Sybil and Marcel enjoyed him but didn't believe him. Kate did, and, as she said afterwards, 'fell about laughing.' Round about midnight Dekker was sprawling under a single sheet—it was a warm night—reading *Kim*, the brigadier having spread Kipling throughout the house. A slight noise at the door disturbed him, and then he saw that Kate, wearing a light dressing gown over a nightdress, had entered his room, though not a word had passed between them on this subject.

'You see, I'm keeping my promise,' she began, trying for a cool easy style but her voice wobbling a little. 'This is the *beautiful welcome* I said you'd have.'

'It's all that—and more—'

'Is it? But now—wretched female that I am—I'm asking myself if it's all that beautiful. We always feel somehow we're a great treat—but then start wondering why.'

'Come here—and stop wondering. Aren't you my own

[134]

beautiful Kate—found and miserably lost—and then found again?'

'Oh—Tom—darling.'

And then of course she was in his arms and they were kissing and kissing. Finally, he whispered, 'I wouldn't put it past Aunt Sybil to butt in. Better lock the door.'

'I did.'

Let us leave them, hoping that imagination and heart came into it and stayed with it through many a time of trial and stress and sudden misunderstandings, belonging both to our exile from Eden and to the peculiar demands of the English Way of Life.